BUG-STOMPERS OF THE
21ST CENTURY

Terry L. Vinson

BUG-STOMPERS OF THE
21ST CENTURY

DOUBLE DRAGON

Prologue

Run Like Hell...The Prequel

*Unreal...surreal...inconceivable...far-fetched.
Pick a cliché, any cliché...but facts are facts, even
in the light of complete, unabashed insanity. How
can something that damn big...bulky as a tractor-
trailer with legs no less...possibly see fit to pursue
little old insignificant me cross-country like a
starved wolf sniffing out a cornered rabbit? Talk
about your 'if it weren't for bad luck I'd have no
luck at all' scenario, this shit is utterly ridiculous.
Not that I had a slew of choices at the time, but I
picked this damn sewer drain mainly for its limited
size, thus what I considered a safe escape route-out
of sight, out of scent...or so I thought. As usual, it
never pays to think.*

*Ahhh, but I shouldn't be the least bit
surprised...it isn't as if this latest in a series of bad
breaks transpired all at once. Pondering on it, the
entire trek's been a real pisser. Why should it
switch gears just because I'm above ground instead
of that flaming pit that's the source of the whole
nightmarish shebang?*

*Worst of all, we managed to stroll right into a
textbook booby-trap from the word go, and they call
humans the smartest species. Well, such egotistical,
cock-sure theories are made to be
broken...sometimes it's just a matter of time...and
really, really bad timing (laughs). Most intelligent
my ass...more like lambs to the proverbial*

5

slaughter, one and all. All our so-called experience and job-related knowledge meant exactly squat, as did the modern techno-pesticide weapons that were supposed to save our collective rear-ends if faced with such a freaky scenario. Might as well have been fighting 'em off with a can of Raid...or maybe chunked a box of Combat baits into the hive for all the good Pretty Boy Floyd's experimental armory toys did us.

The drain reeks of excrement, ammonia, mildew.

Then again, fighting off my gag reflex is definitely a minor annoyance at the moment. I get the feeling this whole sick-fuck scenario is gonna conclude resembling one of those classic Hollywood sci-fi bug flicks, only with no happy ending in sight, no sir. The planet as a whole will be these ugly SOB's oyster. A nesting to end all nestings, so to speak.

Today, New Horizons sub-division...tomorrow, the World! Like I said...what a pisser.

Lord, it's hard to believe such an abomination really exists.

If I hadn't seen it, seem them, with my own eyes. One thing's for damned certain, no matter what the outcome-the pest control business is in for one major league overhaul. The days of the one percent pesticide, ninety-nine percent water mix in the old B&G have gone the way of the cordless phone and cable TV.

Shit...running out of gas big-time-no wonder...legs feel like they've been shoved through a wood chipper. Main thing is not to dwell on it.

Have to maintain focus here. Just...keep on trucking...rockin' and rollin'...take it one step...or limp...at a time 'til I reach pay-dirt-wherever the hell that might be.

Think of the others...how they...how they perished as honorably as one can while fighting a foe that simply refuses to die. Think...think of Beth. Yeah, that's it. If I'm roughly half the trooper that sweet Bethy was, I'll find a way. She sure as hell would've.

Lungs on the verge of imploding-heartbeat pounding on my chest cavity like a jackhammer...all I can think about is how good it would feel just to lay down and sleep for a year or three. Not sure of the distance stretched between us, but I sure as hell can't allow that hungry bitch to get within pinching distance in case I happen to stumble along the way. Moreover, I've got a sinking feeling the two of us ain't alone in or outside this here intestinal tin-can. With that in mind, a half- million ravenous storm-troopers hot on one's heels has a way of bringing out that extra gear you never knew you possessed. That and the mental image of being buried alive by their masses as they chew you into meatball puree. All the way to the bone marrow, baby. I've seen what those merciless little bastards can do to the human body in a relatively short span of time. Seen it up close and waaaay too personal in the past half-hour, in fact. Wish like hell I could erase the memory, but that ain't likely in this or any other lifetime. To quote the obvious, it wasn't at all pleasant nor pretty. Soooo, just keep the mind focused and maintain the stamina level. Can't be more than another fifty yards or so, then I'll poke my head topside and search out an authority figure of some kind-for whatever good that'll do.

Hate to bring it up, much less dwell on it, but a few million lives just might hang in the balance depending on how quick I can produce a suitable warning. Shit, if they only knew their very futures lay in the hands of a limping, beaten-down, near-psychotic pest control tech from East Virginia, I get the feeling the majority would be bending down to kiss their own butt-cheeks sayonara right about now. If so, I can only pray I've got enough gas left in the motivational tank to make 'em regret such negative thinking. Yeah, that's it…something to keep my mind occupied even as the body falls apart at the seams…pray to a higher power that this ain't the end after all. Pray and keep moving…yep-that's the plan-just concentrate, keep on truckin', and don't…stop… praying…

BUG OUT, PART ONE

Mysterious Benefactor

Day One: The Initial In-Brief (*Translation*: The Initial Offer)

Location: New Horizons Corporation Headquarters, New Horizon, Ohio (formerly Davidson, Ohio-once infamous as the location of South Cleveland's most notorious project housing units)

Date: September 17th of the year two-thousand sixteen

As if to validate his well-publicized persona of erratic, borderline psychotic behavior, Gil '*Doctor Death*' Braggs entered the room dancing a wild jig while decked out in full 'MD' regalia, complete with stethoscope, ankle-length lab coat, and mirrored hand-band. Just as he neared the conference table, we all watched with a mixture of bland curiosity and mild disgust as he bent down and scooped something off the slickly waxed floor. In lifting the wriggling object towards the fluorescent lighting above, he slowly separated the fingers grasping the mystery item before turning to us wearing a comically warped grin. He cupped the medium-sized German cockroach in his palm like a small child gently cradling a prized pet before quickly whipping his head back around and tossing it between parted lips. The muffled crunching noises that followed were mercifully drowned out by the round of grunts and guffaws that followed.

Clearly annoyed by the gatherings lack of enthusiasm of his prop-comic act, Braggs took a seat without further fanfare. Obviously, the art of verbal exchange wasn't the man's strong point. Then again, if industry scuttlebutt was even partially factual, 'Doctor Death' and his many minions (forced to dress in similar medical garb) had become a major player in So Cal, Washington State and Oregon, opening branches in as many as eighteen cities. Celebrated nut-job, court jester indeed- seemed more like 'crazy as a fox' status to yours truly.

Twelve seats were filled within the next half-hour, the entire group facing a small burnt oak stage and similarly styled podium. In looking about, I recognized most of the others from various internet ads. Always pays to recognize the enemy in this business, and I'm not referring just to the insect prey from which we make our living.

In fact, considering the plethora of elephantine egos present, it was becoming crystal clear that one stood head and shoulders above all others as King Megalomaniac himself. Yes siree Bob, that dubious distinction belonged to one Virgil 'The Cleaner' Hobbs, three-time Exterminator of the Year as voted by the USPS (United States Pesticide Suppliers) and self-proclaimed 'Intercity Eradicator' for his hand-picked teams 'miraculous' clean-up of Philly's Southside projects during the Crimson Termite swarms of two-thousand fifteen. Just listening to the man prattle on about his own unsurpassed greatness was beginning to twist my gut, and from the sour expressions worn by those around me, the feeling appeared to be mutual. Definitely brought to mind an old twentieth century joke, late nineteen seventies if I'm correct, as in *'pull the cord on the Virgil Hobbs doll and it tells you how good it is.'*

Personally, it had taken less than five full minutes in the man's ultra-cocky, overbearing presence to garner my vote as Prince Prick amongst even the *stiffest* of competition. Painful but true, the casual observer might well have considered our little gathering to be that of a group of pampered, overpaid, self- important professional athletes discussing past playing field heroics-or perhaps even a gaggle of former high-ranking military officers regaling one another with the type of glorified, overblown war stories normally reserved for bargain- basement techno-ebook novels.

"Damn Virg, you housing a pair of artificial lungs or is it that ya simply don't *require* a breathin' pause in-between spoutin' such a heaping, healthy pile of self-adulating horseshit?"

Virgil refused to acknowledge the comment, much less its originator, pretending instead to wipe a clump of invisible dust from the sewn-on patch of his immaculately pressed uniform shift.

"Yep, same old Virg. House plants possess a better sense of humor." This time, Hobbs did at least turn and scowl at the man sitting a few chairs over to his right, curling his lips like a growling canine before huffing loudly and facing front once again.

"Same old *Cloudy*," he finally whispered, though loud enough to overhear in the relative silence,"mouth nearly as big as the dustbowl state he calls home."

Scuttlebutt was that Gaven McCloud, AKA 'The Texas Terminator' had once upon a time shared route time with Virgil Hobbs, though I'd heard wildly varied locations mentioned-everywhere from East Philly to Little Rock to Cheyenne, Wyoming. Needless to say, I wasn't nearly interested enough to dig about for clarification, and it seemed the feeling was mutual among all present. Alas, verification of such useless tidbits about our fellow Exterminators wasn't necessary. I couldn't give a Norway Rat's freshly lain turd about anyone's past, present or future lives. The roomful of rogue pest control tech's I shared space with only cared about two things at present time: the mission and the money.

Cut and dry, as it always was in this nasty little business. Nature of the bug…er, beast, I'm afraid. Shelve the personalities-leave all personal problems and inter- personal squabble at the door. No one gets involved in deep-sixing the world's bug population for the glory of it, and it sure as hell isn't the life-long friendships in a business long-legendary for its massive turnover rate in personnel. Just show me some bugs to stomp and then the money, baby, in *precisely* that order.

I heard Beth sigh a chair over, reaching up with both hands to massage each temple through her latest hairdo, a dark-maroon, spiked job that resembled something from one of those virtual reality Sci-Fi video games. As if the jade- shaded scorpion tattoo on her forehead or the newly implanted, titanium-based fingernails adorning each slender digit wasn't enough in terms of attention getters. Ah well, the girl had never been accused of being shy. Sweet Bethy possessed the physique of a back-alley Tai Juk Do fighter and the profanity-laced vocabulary of a veteran street vamp. No wonder I'd fallen for her so damn hard all those years ago. Definitely my kinda woman, minus the demure, subservient qualities all guys still secretly fantasize about. Talk about your fictional traits. Still, classic Holly-weird flicks remind us that such women did exist at one time. Please your man. Greet him at the door with a frosty brew while wearing an adoring smile and the flimsiest see – through nightly imaginable. Yep, must've been the ticket alright, if such a Shangri-La did indeed ever truly exist. Personally, I never witnessed a trace of such behavior in my own numerous, mostly fruitless affairs. The bug-stomping business isn't exactly pegged as the most romantic of career choices. Ah yes, the aroma of BO and pesticide may be considered many things, but an aphrodisiac definitely isn't one of 'em.

"Jesus, what's the hold up? Let's get this show on the road already. Time is money, for shits sake…" Beth grunted, flexing meticulously toned biceps while leaning back to stretch out both her bare, darkly tanned arms.

"You got that right, sweets. Free plane ride and hotel digs be damned, somebody needs to step forward and spills the beans on this little mystery," echoed Luther *'The Ebony Assassin'* Bohannon in a voice so deep and gravelly it was almost comical, though I'll be damned if anyone present possessed the cohunes to express a similar opinion with even the most inconspicuous of giggles.

I saw Beth openly cringe at the 'sweets' remark, though she wisely chose not to challenge a man whose overall stature was akin to that of amedium-sized moving van. No doubt Bohannon's well-noted past as both a pro circuit wrestler and internet porn star aided in enhancing his own legend as a man not to be trifled with. Still, it was one of the few times I witnessed such hesitation in a woman who normally regarded such blatant chauvinism as nothing less than a declaration of war.

"Patience, people, patience. Have faith in the powers that be," a new, notably more refined voice chimed in with a noted British twang,"I'm sure there's a justifiable reason that twelve of the World's most celebrated exterminators have been called together for noontime tea.

In due time. All in due time," spewed forth the senior member of the invited guests, one Delbert '*Clean Sweep*' Prescott, he of the eight 'Exterminator of the Year Awards' of Great Britain fame before relocating to the US East Coast following the new millennium.

"Ah, patience my ass, old man. Took me six blessed hours to fly here from Jersey, counting flight delays. Whatever it's about…it damn well better be worth the trouble," blurted Brad '*Killer Bee*' Bedford in a whiny, nasal moan that was as annoying as it was cringe-inducing. Easily the youngest of those present, Bedford was not without his own fast-building rep in the industry. Quite the eccentric group-the 'Dirty Dozen' of the pest control industry, one might say. Not really sure if I felt honored or downright embarrassed to be counted amongst their ranks. Regardless, there I sat, along with my former live-in lover and business partner of the past nine years. In Beth's case, it wasn't necessary to ask for an assessment of the situation. I could read her expression like the weathered pages of a well-worn paperback. Ticked off scowls and perturbed moans aside, she was on the verge of orgasmic delight at the prospect of something new and out of the ordinary-in other words, *anything* to escape the daily grind and mundane universe that made up the whole of commercial pest control.

"Not to worry, Mister Bedford," still another alien voice rang out from the rear of the conference room,"I'm quite certain our impending offer of employment will soon sooth the brittle nerves of all involved."

The dude was young; painfully so, probably no more than thirty on the outside. With his oil-slick, close-cropped do and shiny-slick black three-piece suit, he looked every bit the stereotypical preppy CEO type. The room instantly filled with the scent of high-end cologne straight from Sachs Fifth's 'Elite' on-line catalog, the type that requires an upfront fee in the thousands just to browse. It was a sickly sweet aroma I'd become accustomed to while treating homes belonging to the upper crust of society. Striding to the front of the room with two similarly decked out cronies on either side ('hired muscle' Beth had whispered, nodding my way), the man's very walk exhumed arrogance, just as his snooty, sarcastic tone had earmarked his lifelong standing among the privileged few.

"Let's hope so, slick," Luther Bohannon barked, struggling as not to shatter the woefully undersized chair parked beneath his massive bulk. Swear to God, the man's neck was as thick as my waist, no small feat considering my recent rediscovery of carbohydrates.

"I'm a busy man. Too busy to have my precious time wasted, know what I mean?"

Slick turned to face us wearing a smug, Cheshire-cat grin that screamed insincerity, crossing his arms across his chest as his two stoic cohorts took up position a few steps to his rear.

"Understood, Mister Bohannon sir, and I consider it a safe assumption that each of you feel a similar apprehension as to the rather…vague invitation that led you here this day."

Gaven McCloud laughed aloud, tossing his shiny bald head back like a baying wolf. His thick, walrus mustache bounced about like a live caterpillar.

"Vague? Hell son, that's puttin' it mildly. Gotta say, if not for the free ride, digs and cash advance, this old boy would be smack-dab in the middle of his annual early summer gnat slaughter. As it is, I left the keys to the kingdom in the hands of a tech staff I trust about as far as I can heave a dump truck. In other words, spit it out as quickly as those gloss-coated lips can manage so I can get back to day to day operations."

"Here, here, old boy, by all means please educate us," Delbert Prescott added with a mild clap, igniting a loud murmur between several others sitting to my rear.

Shoving his chair back from the conference table with a loud screech, Virgil Hobbs then stood and slammed the palms of both hands against the table, causing everyone present save perhaps the unflappable Gaven McCloud to flinch as if back-handed.

"Would you people just clam up and give the man a chance to speak, for Christ's sake? I for one am shamed by the childish behavior on display from my…so-called peers."

After a moments silence, McCloud cackled aloud. Beth and I exchanged grins as Hobbs retook his seat amidst a spattering of giggles.

"Always the drama queen, right Virg? A real spotlight magnet you are. Some things never change…" McCloud concluded as the head suit cleared his throat and prepared to enlighten us.

"Gentleman…and lady…" he began, glancing overhead at some unseen object while wringing his hands like the expert salesman I was sure he most certainly was,"allow me to place squarely on the table, so to speak, what might well be the most potentially lucrative offer you will *ever* bare witness to in your chosen profession…"

BUG OUT, PART TWO

The Grand Scheme

"First off, allow me to introduce myself," Slick
continued, his muscle-bound cohorts departing the
room as if on cue,"my name is Floyd C. Garrison. I
serve as the Executive Vice-President for Property
Acquisitions and Community Replenishment for the
Net-Scan Corporation. Long title, I know, but only
the good Lord knows the daily challenges I'm pitted
against each and every day simply to justify the
salary connected to it."

Several of my peers snickered sarcastically, no
doubt thinking along the same lines as myself-that
the salary 'Pretty Boy Floyd' there referred to might
well surpass all our annual incomes combined.

"As many of you may or may not know, the
New Horizons Corporation won the bid on the old
Metro Davidson Housing Projects sixteen months
ago. This was soon followed by the renaming of the
entire Davidson town-ship to its present name, New
Horizons, the conglomerate who now owns my
employer, Net-Scan."

"Yeah, your company and half the free world,
pal," Brad Bedford screeched, sounding more like a
grade-school punk with a busted I-Pod than one of
the twelve elite exterminators on the planet,"NH's
monopoly makes Wal-Mart seem like a chain of
backstreet lemonade stands."

"Be that as it may…" Garrison started to
resume, only to be cut off at the knees by my
erstwhile partner and former better-half, who loved

18

nothing better than diving in head-first at the first sign of a verbal skirmish, no matter the subject.

"Yeah, you gotta own some stainless steel crotch-bags to step in and alter the letterhead of an entire city with your company logo, man," she crooned through a tight smile I knew didn't hold a tint of actual good humor. My girl Beth despised all things political and big business, most notably on those many occasions when the two were so obviously in cahoots. Still, despite the underlining grimness of her building rant, I found myself fighting back a loud cackle at her use of 'crotch-bags'.

"I mean, what's next anyhow? *Walgreens*, Minnesota? *Yahoo*, Kansas?

Google Fucking California?"

Pretty Boy Floyd cleared his throat numerous times while waiting for the laughter to subside, a fine mist of perspiration beginning to coat his forehead.

"Um, well, I'm not at all qualified to speak of the New Horizons versus Davidson City Counsel case, that is…it's not relevant to what. . . to the offer…. um…" he began before pausing in mid-babble to motion to the two bodyguards, who had re-entered the conference room toting what resembled one of the newer, state-of-the-art HRID (Hologram Re-Imaging Displays) units, along with a mini-tripod brace and several sealed but unlabeled disc containers.

"Ah, I see the show and tell portion of our presentation has arrived," Garrison grinned, obviously relieved at the sudden intrusion.

19

"Now I can begin to answer the questions that really matter, folks. Get down to 'brass tax' as our ever-wise forefathers used to say."

Not sure about the others, but I was beginning to think we'd all unwillingly signed up for the same infomercial seminar, minus the cheapie 'free' meal one received for enduring the inevitable sales-spiel.

"I'll be utilizing specific holograms as they pertain, so please bear with me."

Someone farted just as Garrison had paused, a muffled yet obviously powerful butt-bomb that echoed off the solid oak conference chair with a hollow thud. While most, including myself, merely snickered and easily refocused, I thought Gil *'Doctor Death'* Braggs and Brad *'Killer Bee'* Bedford were gonna need oxygen. Took 'em both a full two minutes to regain their adulthood, and even then Bedford would occasionally break into a fit of giggles. Never one to consider toilet humor as the least bit humorous, Beth simply rolled her eyes and remained neutral. As she was often want to say, 'must be a guy thing'.

"If I may continue after that rather unexpected interlude," Garrison resumed, though noticeably a bit red-faced,"we have a lot to cover, people, and though it may sound cliché, it truly is a matter of life and death. Life, death, and potential wealth, actually, and precisely in that order."

"*Now* you got my attention, Slick. By all means, please continue…" announced Luther Bohannon in an impossibly deep baritone, and as if the Commander-in-Chief himself had spoken, all feel instantly silent.

Seemingly reenergized by the big man's verbal 'permission', Pretty Boy Floyd inhaled deeply and visibly relaxed. Have to say, by the time his four to five minute presentation had concluded, I found my jaw had involuntarily unhinged and every short hair I possessed was standing as rigid as porcupine quills.

"Folks, the trouble began almost as soon as the Davidson Housing Projects were torn down to make room for the newly drawn up New Horizons Townhouses. What started as a minor irritation in the success of their completion has since mutated into what can only be described as a living nightmare. In the past several weeks, I've heard the project defined by such words as 'cursed' and 'damned' by powerful men and women of industry-CEO's and company heads whose past successes in the cut-throat world of big business held very little regard for the likes of unbiased fear and superstition.

Then again, from what I've personally witnessed in these past few months, I've had to reevaluate my own beliefs on such crude, uncivilized topics. To wit…"

Now…I'm not saying I'm the toughest hombre to ever strap on a pesticide- rigged exo-skeleton body suit and crawl into a beastie-infested drainpipe carrying only a pen-light and micro-injector, but it still takes a hell of a jolt to drain me pale. As if Garrison's story wasn't grim enough, the accompanying holograms were downright horrifying. Haven't had a 'bout with the Willies that severe since I found myself standing knee-deep in a bore-ant hive a few years back. Fear is relative I guess, but after all, this is coming from a man who's seen his share of gruesomeness in the bug-trade over the past decade. It isn't as if I didn't know from experience that the effects of global warning had created its share of creeping horrors, but if the contents of those holograms *had been* real and not some Hollywood CGI effect, I'd been woefully naïve at the level of said monstrosities. From the overall mood of those around me, the ill-at-ease feelings were hardly mine alone. All the humor, sarcastic or otherwise, had been sucked from the room like cigar smoke via typhoon winds. Beth's usually rosy complexion was chalky-white as she tapped those metallic nails against the table without a hint of rhythm. Worst yet, and certainly more telling, Luther *the bad- ass* Bohannon was chomping at his fingernails like a spooked kid eye-balling a particularly scary scene from a classic horror flick. Hell, even the two top Court- Jesters present, Misters Bedford and Braggs, had fell as sullen as a pair of twin morticians. It's a stretch, I know, but that was the single silver lining. Otherwise, I could've done without the grisly particulars. Sure would've found sleep a bit easier in the nights that followed.

Amazing to me still that the national, not to mention local, media hadn't been all over this story like dung beetles on a fresh, steaming pile of cow pies. Just goes to show the power behind the whole New Horizons takeover of central Ohio. Obviously tons of political pull, not to mention boat-loads of

22

cash, can quell even the juiciest tale of mystery, injustice, and grisly death.

Once the projects had been targeted for destruction and the two- thousand or so low-to-*nil* income inhabitants essentially given the bum's rush to oblivion-city, the big-wigs at New Horizons wasted little time before whistling for the wrecking ball and a veritable army of bulldozers. The cries of community leaders fell on stone-deaf ears as what had been labeled 'Phase One' of the New Horizons renovation of the downtown district carried on as scheduled. Took a seventy-man crew less than five full work days to flatten thirty-three buildings housing nearly seven-hundred apartments. Talk about 'prioritizing', it never ceases to amaze how effortlessly the system can be raped over by the rich and powerful. Five blessed days and the city formerly known as Davidson saw its homeless population increase by about four-hundred percent. Only goes to show how greed will kick needs ass every damn time. Never in history has the gap between the have and have-nots been as wide. As spacious as the great Mississippi, brother, and growing father apart with every national election that goes by the boards.

Anyhow, it seems the magical renovation hit some serious snags right off the bat, most of 'em related to the projects former inhabitants and their refusal to accept such treatment lying down.

There'd been several incidents of sabotage as the construction crews had began their demolition, everything from the theft of equipment to homemade bomb explosions that severely damaged

23

the same. Worst had been a timed pipe-bomb detonation set inside the cab of a skip-loader that not only killed its operator, but also triggered a series of flash-fires that took the lives of three others on site.

Not all snags were man-made however, as a series of mild earthquakes damaged several foundations, triggering a week-long delay in new construction as necessary repairs took priority. Damned if I knew that central Ohio was such a 'hot-bed' for quakes. Like so many world-wide abnormalities, chalk it up to the 'GW' effect…that's Global Warming, for those unfamiliar.

As for the human threat, the corporation turned to private sector security to oversee the property and protect the site workers, hiring a firm out of nearby Cleveland with a reputation for dealing with such cowardly, guerilla tactics with swift, merciless, brute force. According to Pretty Boy Floyd, it wasn't long before all was peace and quiet on the demolition front once again; a few bruises, broken bones and lacerations not withstanding. He said once trouble did rear its ugly head once again, it had little to do with former project malcontents tossing beer bottles, sitting off M-80's or even local community leaders pushing for human rights and *everything* to do with the insect world.

It'd been in the final days of clean-up, when two-dozen ton-and-a half trucks had descended onto the grounds to fill their beds with crushed rubble and splintered wood, that crew members commenced to mysteriously vanish. He wasn't talking about walking off the job either, as in voluntary resignations.

Nope, these guys-mostly dump-truck drivers or bulldozer operators-all went 'poof' in broad daylight without ever providing a forwarding address. All in all, seven of 'em disappeared in three days from the grounds of the former Metro Davidson Housing Projects. You could almost hear the theme music from that old Sci-Fi show, Twilight Zone, blaring in the background, man. I swear, by the time Pretty Boy Floyd turned to the holograms to supplement the plot, it was like he was standing in a circle telling us ghost stories by campfire light.

The holograms in question, at least the ones whose imagery shot straight into the marrow of this boy's bones, displayed several of the missing crew members upon their bodies being discovered several days after the fact. Might be more apt to say what *remained* of said bodies. Tattered scraps of flesh and hollowed out bones, the majority hardly recognizable as human. Wasn't 'til the company brought out a team of forensic eggheads that the remains were officially identified as three of the missing crew, and even then it was via the age- old technique of matching any surviving teeth with old x-ray records. We were shown holograms of all three victims as they were found, though it still prays on my mind how Pretty Boy Floyd and his New Horizons flunkies got their mitts on what had to be confidential police evidence. Again, it's all about having friends in high places, not to mention an unlimited well of funds to dip into and delve out to the 'right' people.

Now, I've seen what a nest of Skin-Bore Ants or Bloated-Belly Scorpions can do, not to mention the irreversible damage a few dozen Jamaican Cannibal Roaches can inflict upon exposed flesh, but this was different. This was on a higher plain of gruesome. This was downright barf-inducing, at least to those weak of stomach in viewing such matters. Then again, it wasn't as if Floyd Garrison and the corporate hierarchy didn't realize exactly to whom they were divulging such visceral imagery. Nor were they ignorant in the realization that those present could not only ID the probable mortis operandi of said imagery, but also possess the knowledge to plot the impending demise of those responsible.

I heard Gaven McCloud whisper, apparently to himself and no one else in particular, something to the effect of "Ain't no lack of suspects when it comes to the killin' part. Large-Mouth Daddy-Long legs or a Violin-Recluse, maybe even a Jagged-legged Centipede, but none of the above are noted for stickin' around to mutilate the corpse for kicks. More than likely a dozen or so of those mutated Norway rats-I hear they've been spotting 'em as thick-bodied as your average English Bulldog down near Mexico way."

"Yep, could be," Beth followed up with a disgusted sneer while eyeing the hologram of the last victim through a tight squint,"Jesus...poor dude's husk looks like it was sucked dry from the inside."

The rep from Great Britain then chimed in with his usual high level of snootiness. Still, the man's rep alone rated him considerable respect in my book.

"No so fast, good people. Surely you've heard of the flesh-consuming cockroach that hails from the Caribbean. Why, a nesting of those vile creatures have been known to strip an exposed cadaver in less than six hours."

Mumblings and grumblings went back and forth for several minutes, and I could see the sparkle in Pretty Boy Floyd's eyes at the sudden barrage of interest, however disjointed and disagreeable. No doubt it was just the reaction he and the corporation were hoping for. Obviously, these rich SOB's had reached the end of their collective ropes in terms of a solution, *any* solution, and we were their chosen savors, a hand-picked squadron of efficiency experts that could easily be had for a price. Twenty-first Century bug-stompers, that was us in a nutshell. No doubt those stuffed shirts considered our little group not only the most eccentric yet proven collection of pest eradicators on the planet, but also their last best chance to secure a multi-million dollar investment. Can't say I wasn't flattered by the invite, no matter the level of self-preservation and selfishness involved. I mean, being considered one of the twelve best in any field was pretty damn impressive, especially in a business where there are approximately sixteen-thousand new certifications issued each year nationwide. All that said, I recall being a tad bit embarrassed that I didn't have a single blessed clue what had turned those three poor bastards into shredded steak tarter. Far as I could draw from my ten plus years of executing mass-murder on the insect world, there wasn't a bug flying, crawling, or squirming that could inflict such carnage. Then again, the predators of old had experienced quite the evolutionary upgrade since Global Warning had kicked into overdrive, and it wasn't beyond the realm of possibility. Certainly the stuffed suits weren't thinking animal attack, or else it would've been a dozen big-game *hunters* sitting around that conference table instead.

As Garrison's story progressed, it became clear that additional evidence arose in the days following that would permanently cross all animal and human suspects off the list, hence the callout for pest control's elite to join the fray.

Seems the powers that be at New Horizons had done a bang-up job at concealing those first deaths from the local media, dare such grave reports delay construction. If the bad news had ended there, chances are condos might've gone up on time, a mere two months after the projects had been leveled. After all, Horizons had hired on not one...not two...but three of the top-rated construction crews in the country, one of which had been contracted out of Southern California, no less. Rumor had it, unsubstantiated of course, that several sports and entertainment biz big-wigs had already signed on the bottom line to obtain said condos. Being that the three bedroom jobs had been priced at just under a cool million and a half, such scuttlebutt wasn't too hard to swallow, despite the fact we were talking about central freakin' Ohio and not Beverly Hills, Colorado Springs or Vegas. Strange the areas of the country that suddenly became posh once most folks fled the south and southwest a decade back. Sure never would've envisioned a former slum area as the future 'place to be' for all the beautiful people looking to escape the limelight.

Anyhow, things didn't exactly go as planned in terms of keeping on schedule. According to Pretty Boy F, they'd barely laid the stone foundations when more crew members came up missing, usually from the skeleton crews forced to work the night shift. Didn't exactly require a brain surgeon nor astrophysicist to spot the pattern, no sir. Hell, even your everyday working Joe knows that bugs are infinitely more active at night. Bingo. Mystery solved even before some hotshot entomologist flown in from the Big Apple confirmed the first three deaths as insect-related (so much for the Giant Norway Rat theories). This time though, no remains surfaced. Not as much as a shred of flesh or single bone fragment.

A three-day work stoppage was announced, during which time New Horizons hired on still another security firm-this one hailing from the Big Apple no less-to patrol the grounds. Even though Garrison didn't elaborate, I can only speculate that the suits might've figured on foul play of a more human nature, as in guerilla warfare with a street-wise twist.

Less than a week later, the security firm packed up and headed back to NYC minus four of their assigned patrol officers, all of 'em having performed the self-same vanishing act. Guess it was damned obvious by then that all the M. I. A action had little to do with disgruntled former project inhabitants taking revenge on 'the man'. In the meantime, the 'bug doctor' for hire they'd brought on made quite the discovery inside one of the semi-constructed condo frames. Seems he'd run across what he referred to as a 'massive slug trail' leading from inside the hollowed-out living room to the dirt-covered back yard area.

At this point, Garrison had paused as to catch his breath and allow the hologram image to fill our collective eyes. Damned if that wasn't exactly what it looked like, too; a shiny, moistened path leading from the center of the room to between a pair of wooden two-by-fours and out onto a concave mound of dirt and clay. Sure, we'd all seen 'em before, countless times. Seen 'em on stone and brick walls and concrete and wooden decks, usually more frequently spotted started in early spring and up until late summer turned to fall in the warmer climes. Only difference was, these particular markings weren't the typical half to one inch wide-oh hell no, this queer looking SOB looked to be more in the vicinity of one to one and a half *feet* wide. As in twelve to eighteen inches. Not your average, ordinary snail-trail, no siree. Not by a long shot.

"Jumping Jack Flash, what in hell could've left that oil slick behind?" I heard Gil 'Doctor Death' Braggs spout, leaning up and onto the conference

30

table 'til it looked as though he were literally trying to crawl into the image for a better look-see.

"Oh, I dunno...yo momma perhaps?" Brad Bedford quipped in response, though with a serious lack of conviction. Far as I know, no one even cracked a smile. Alas, the group had yet to regain even a semblance of the good humor of earlier.

I saw Beth raise a hand just as the hologram faded and Garrison had opened his mouth to resume. Girl rarely missed an opportunity to stir the pot. Just one of the many things I loved about her.

"So the general consensus is that whatever left that goo-trail is our mystery assassin?"

Wiping his brow with the back of one hand, Garrison sighed deeply and stared briefly down at his high-gloss dress shoes before responding. Once he did, both his expression and tone were dipped in equal amounts of sarcasm. It was obvious the man wasn't at all used to be interrupted. Cocky little shit. No doubt born with a silver foot planted firmly in his mouth, or at the very least a gold-plated pacifier.

"Why yes, Miss Cambridge, that is *precisely* the consensus. I was just about to divulge that traces of the same...goo, as you called it, was found on the earlier three victims. It was discovered to be non-manmade, that is...insect in origin."

"Well, that sure cuts down the suspects, now don't it?" Gaven McCloud responded wryly while providing his shiny, bald dome a vigorous rubdown with both palms,"all we gotta do then is obtain a pee sample from all sixteen million bug species on planet Earth and match 'em up with that load of butt-slime and we got our murderer!"

31

Despite the man's gruff exterior and non-stop dialogue of the smart-ass variety, I couldn't help but like 'im. Guess I always felt a kinship with the malcontents of the world, though I never truly counted myself among their lofty ranks.

"Mister   McCloud...people..."   Garrison pleaded, raising both hands palms up like a preacher attempting to calm a restless flock,"if I could just be allowed to continue without further interruption. I...that is, Doctor Will Bumgartner will be arriving to answer all your...technical questions in just a bit."

After a few snickers at the mere mention of the good 'bug' doctor's name, the room again fell silent. Still, the overall mood of unease hadn't faded a single iota. If anything, it had increased a decibel or two in light of the unexpected horror show we'd been subjected to. Can't speak of anyone but yours truly, but I had a feeling everyone present was straining like hell to maintain a cool exterior throughout. As Garrison resumed, and eventually concluded, I have to confess to feeling a beach-ball sized knot forming at the center of my chest. As the story progressed, I can't honestly report any shrinkage of said growth. Sad truth is, that bad boy would experience one hell of a scary growth spurt in the aftermath.

"...as for the monetary offer, folks," he concluded with a shit-gnawing grin and the wink of an eye,"let's just say it's an unprecedented amount for what mostly will amount to a single days work."

At that point, no one dared fart aloud, much less interrupt the offer we'd all been waiting to hear.

"We, that is the New Horizons Corporation, will compensate each man or woman…" he paused, no doubt for stage dramatics sake if not to fuel his own egotistical urgings,"one-hundred thousand dollars in cash. All we ask in return is a danger and pest-free site for which to return our construction crews."

"One-hundred…thousand…" Virgil babbled first as the rest of us were still exchanging disbelieving glances,"how many *retreats* we talking about here? I mean, no way your talking a single treatment for that kind of green, right?"

Garrison looked positively insulted by the query, but recovered with the skill of a veteran's salesman, his excitable tone never wavering. Personally, I trusted this preppy clown about as far as I could heave 'im. Then again, it was damn near impossible to ignore the hefty number he'd tossed out there-like a meaty bone to a starving hound. In our most profitable year in the business, that being three years back, Beth and I had cleared just under one-hundred ten grand. That said, it took working twelve hour days six days a week just to reach that particular tax bracket. Plus which, the last two years had seen that hefty sum cut damn near in-half. There'd been several reasons for the decline, not the least of which was the glut of new companies that had opened up shop since severe climate changes had spawned a fresh batch of mutated bug-beasties to deal with.

Yep, there was no denying the man was dangling quite the worm-heavy hook our way, one that made me temporarily bypass the potential dangers involved.

"Once Doctor Bumgartner assures us that all traces of...imminent danger have passed, Mister Hobbs, you will be cleared of all obligation. How many...retreats as you referred to them, this takes will be determined by the good doctor's findings."

Leaning his massive bulk forward, Luther Bohannon leaned his bloated forearms onto the table before clearing his throat-the effect of which was the equivalent of small-arms fire echoing inside constrictive cave-walls.

"So correct me if I'm wrong here, Slick, but you're offering the aforementioned amount to each of us individually, though were supposed to work as a 'team' to find and eradicate the threat."

"The 'team' thing is purely your own choice, Mister Bohannon. We don't care how the mission is accomplished or which of you is most responsible for its success. Regardless, shares will be equal."

Delbert Prescott snorted loudly to my left, crossing his arms and throwing his head back as if somebody had just snagged the edges of his 'dandy' mustache before pulling and snapping 'em back like rubber bands. A real card, Dandy Delbert. Just loved the way that 'bloke' talked.

"So we can work individually to solve your problem, then? This isn't some bloody boy scout nature study?"

"As I've said, Mister Prescott, work together or separately. We have no set rules. We simply want the threat thwarted...better yet, permanently eliminated."

34

Beth shot me a look that was a weird hybrid indeed, equal parts tentative elation and blatant distrust.

"Thwarted?" she whispered my way through a comically warped grin,"did that corporate weasel really just say *thwarted?*"

"Beginning to feel like we're living in a graphic novel, babe," I responded with a shrug.

Rolling her eyes seductively, she then reached over and lightly pinched my left shoulder.

"You got that right, Ace, a gory, graphic tale whose ending has yet to be written."

"So whip out the contracts already, Slick," Luther Bohannon blurted with a wide grin, flashing a shiny gold grill in all its gaudy glory.

Virgil Hobbs clapped his hands excitedly, though remaining in character otherwise while steadfastly refusing to reveal a facial expression least the skin thereabout crack and peel away from the effort.

"I second that motion. Let's make it official."

His pearly-whites bared like the devoted company man he most surely was, Garrison paced the stage several times while nodding his head from side to side.

"It isn't as though I, that is, the corporation, isn't thrilled with the exuberance you've displayed for accepting the mission at hand, but I'm afraid it isn't quite as simple as all of you lining up to sign on the dotted line."

As if on cue, every forehead in the joint creased in confusion. Not surprisingly, Gaven McCloud was the first to speak up.

"Meaning *what*, Slick? Kinda late in the game to be backtracking, ain't it?"

"Yes, it most certainly would be, Mister McCloud, if indeed that was myintention," came the smug reply, those sparkling pearlies vanishing only long enough for the spoken words to shoot through. I never understood how such folks could freeze-frame a fake grin for such lengthy periods and never appear the least bit strained. Must be one of those talents you're either born with or your not. Scary to think one could be trained for such behavior. Such is the artificially flavored, cut-throat world of big business. No place for pussies.

"The thing is, we cannot make such a lucrative offer to all twelve present here today. In fact, those numbers must be cut in half before the operational phase can proceed."

"Son, I gotta tell ya…I ain't used to having to audition for a job…*any* job," McCloud crooned, puffing out his chest like the King Rooster in a henhouse,"you want the best, I offer the best. You turn me back, its de-fi-nite-ly your loss, Hoss."

"Jesus, McCloud, you got brass balls calling *me* egotistical," Virgil Hobbs snickered, coming dangerously close to cracking a smile in the process. Let me rehash something I might've already hinted at early on: though I'd never personally made the man's acquaintance, Virgil *'The Cleaner'* Hobbs was one dude I knew for dead certainty that I didn't like. We've all met such folks as life progresses. There's no concrete reason for the initial dislike, no real justification, but you simply know it from the first time they swim into view or their lips first part to speak. Hobbs was one such hombre in my personal black book of 'pricks to avoid'. Actually, from the man's less-than-amiable rep, I had a feeling his name was stitched in many such journals nationwide.

McCloud paused thoughtfully, propping his chin atop a clinched fist.

"Why, I never speak of inflated ego when I mention your name, Virg. Naw, the name that most comes to mind would have to be more along the lines of...King Jackass."

"Enough of this juvenile banter," Delbert Prescott huffed, and I could've sworn his Brit twang faded the more agitated he became.

"Tell us then, Mister Garrison, how do we...qualify for the first team, so to speak?"

"Well, to be perfect honest, Mister Prescott," Garrison answered, his perpetual grin briefly resembling a soured grimace,"the first team, as you so aptly put it, had already been pre-chosen long since before your arrival here in our fair city. The thing is, we never considered all twelve of our original line-up would actually agree to the mission. We...figured on eight or nine at the most, which would leave us several...alternates to choose from if the need arose. Seriously, we never dreamed that all of you would take us up on the offer without...some serious reservation. Not after...not after what we've shown you thus far in terms of the dangers involved."

Following still another 'team' double-take, in which the majority present collectively sighed, leaned back, and exchanged a series of awkward glances, all eyes beamed in on a blue-tinted plasma screen that slowly dropped down from the rear of the stage, just beyond the stoic image of our erstwhile employer.

Meantime, Beth couldn't refrain from tossing forth a verbal haymaker just for good measure. I had begun to wonder how long she'd stay tight-lipped amongst all the chatter.

"You offer one-hundred grand for a single days work and are genuinely surprised when a room full of working class stiffs takes you up on it? Man, you've been eating off the finest China for waaaay too long, you know that?"

Garrison simply shrugged in response as the bottom-edge of the flat- screen plasmas kissed the stage floor a few feet to his rear.

"Perhaps you are correct, Miss Cambridge. Regardless, let us now discuss who among you has…made the final cut. In fairness to those who did not, I will cover the reasons for our individual choices."

BUG OUT, PART THREE

And Then There Were Six

"I apologize in advance, good people, if the following appears a bit too close for comfort to Beauty Pageant's of old. My staff had but days to put this together. Nonetheless, we believe the research completed on each of you as individual business men...and woman...was extensive enough to choose the most experienced and potentially efficient team of exterminators ever to serve on a single mission of eradication."

Swear to god, the man's false sincerity and ultra-stilted dialogue was beginning to have its effect on my eyelids, each of which felt as though they were hosting separate anchors of the heavy metal variety.

"No need to blow smoke up our collective asses, Junior," Gaven McCloud spouted, echoing my personal sentiments exactly.

"Just tell us who goes and who stays already."

Clearing his throat while pulling a palm-sized remote from his suit's front left pocket, Garrison no longer appeared the least bit amused.

"Cut to the chase, then. Yes, it does seem that the proper amenities have run bone dry at this point. Very well then, the first member of the team is none other than..."

Activating the remote with the twitch of a thumb, he backed away a step as the blue screen temporarily filled with static before the initial image swam into view.

"As if there was ever any doubt whatsoever," a whiny, grating voice rang out joyfully as his grinning mug greeted us in all its (lets hope intentionally) comedic glory. The photo was obviously lifted from the company website, and featured 'team member' number one standing posed in a victory pose with one booted foot balanced atop the chest-cavity of what was apparently supposed to be a giant-sized Shredder Locust but was clearly just a man lying face-up in a deflated rubber suit. Flashing just beneath the deceased 'pests' lifeless corpse was the slogan 'WE TAKE AN OATH-TO ELIMINATE WHATEVER BUGS YA!"

From there, Garrison provided what the corporation must've deemed the mandatory narrative, which I gotta say came out sounding like some third-tier reality show introducing a forth-rate cast of celebrity wannabes. Little did I know the real embarrassment of the evening had yet to surface.

NAME: Gil Braggs
KNOWN PROFESSIONALLY AS: 'Doctor Death'
SEX/RACE: White Male
BORN: Hawthorne, California
TITLE: Owner, operator of 'Doctor Death's Bug Cemeteries'; sixteen offices located in six western states
AGE: Thirty-four
EXTERMINATOR SINCE: Initial certification as Pest Control Tech on July 19th, two-

thousand five. Licensed and chartered in October, two- thousand eight

MISC NOTES: Certified in six Western states; home office located in Englewood, California. Named California Exterminator of the Year (two-thousand eleven; thirteen; and fifteen)

ON THE PERSONAL SIDE: Single (never married); lists hobbies as 'avid LA Lakers and California Raiders fanatic'. Thus, has attended last two- hundred sixteen Laker home games and maintains a luxury box suite at all Raider home contests. To date, has appeared in over three-hundred local television commercials in all six states where service is available, appearing as his alter-ego, 'Doctor Death'.

P. C (Pest Control) CLAIM TO FAME: Original 'Cemetery' store reportedly lost over four-hundred thousand dollars in its first two years. By fourth year of existence, however, the company claimed three additional branches and a fiscal year profit of just over one million.

"Campy clown," I heard Beth mumble from within a cupped palm."Fat-catting PR genius who probably ain't snuffed out as much as a carpenter ant in years."

I wasn't about to argue with my partner and former better-half. Braggs appeared the type who'd spent the majority of his time perched behind a desk since hitting the big time, chomping donuts and sipping coffee as his hired cronies fleeced a gullible public with half-assed termite inspections-spraying for mostly harmless, if not completely non-existent bugs for the rich-and-infamous in and around the San Fernando Valley. Simply put, I saw the good 'doctor' as being loud of mouth and soft of gut. *Translation:* The prospect of being teamed with such a loud mouthed slacker wasn't exactly blowing my skirt.

"Congratulations, Mister...um, Doctor," Garrison spewed with sickening disingenuousness as Braggs nodded immodestly.

"Alright then, onto team member number two, that being none other than..."

A low clicking sound brought forth image number two, a grainy black and white photo that looked to have been taken from old newsprint.

NAME: Delbert Prescott
KNOWN PROFESSIONALLY AS: 'Clean Sweep'
TITLE: Owner, operator of The 'Clean Sweep Pest Control Agency'; six offices located in and around the Virginia, Washington DC area.
AGE: Fifty-one **SEX/RACE:** White Male
BORN: London, England
EXTERMINATOR SINCE: Initial certification (London, England listed as original licensing city) on May 13th, 1986. Licensed and chartered (in United States) on September 19th, 2000.
MISC NOTES: Earned Exterminator of The Year nod in Great Britain eight years running (1994-2001). Reportedly turned down offers from

five separate U. S. pest control companies and instead started the 'Clean Sweep America' agencies in October 2002. Has since grown to the aforementioned six offices, not counting the four he'd originally founded abroad, for which he still holds the title of CEO and managing partner.

ON THE PERSONAL SIDE: Married for twenty-eight years to Gwendolyn; four children, two grandchildren. Lists sole hobby as 'tending family' and collecting classic American-built sports automobiles (to include late twentieth century models such as the Chevy Corvette, Ford Mustang and Pontiac Firebird). Still actively participates in pest control treatments, most recently in the elimination of a deadly skin-bore ant infestation near Sperryville, Virginia.

P. C (Pest Control) CLAIM TO FAME: Served on Great Britain's parliament as an advisor on matters of urban decay from an entomology standpoint. Officially 'knighted' in the year two-thousand ten for his 'many contributions to the safety and welfare of all Brits and future generations thereof. '

"Sounds like a hands-on bloke," I whispered to Beth, who was eyeing 'Sir' Prescott suspiciously.

"Maybe," she responded, curling a lip seductively, "or it's all PR bullshit to make 'im appear just another grunt for appearances sake. Can't trust those damn englishers. Always having to pull their asses outta the fire, historically- wise."

That's my Bethy. Never trust another living soul until they prove their worth, and even then it's a case by case proposition. Then again, she had a point. I mean, up until New Horizons had decided to pool our collective knowledge into a single working machine, all these people had been our sworn enemies; rivals in a business that had damn much competition as it was from 'guaranteed' over-the-counter pesticide manufacturers and overzealous, low- budgeted homeowners who fought their own fight with ancient pest control remedies better suited for the dark ages. It ain't like we were making friends here. Nope, it was more like…re-evaluating the competition to see who would eventually stroll outta the fire with the least burns.

Still, with his perfectly trimmed 'dandy' mustache curled upwards at the ends, 'high and tight' crew-cut and meticulously ironed uniform (dark red shirt with matching pants, complete with white stripe up the sides of each leg and spit-polished black boots), one couldn't help but assume they were in the presence of a true professional. Man looked trim and fit for his age, as well, and the 'high tea' accent was a pleasant diversion if nothing else.

Besides, despite the fact I wasn't the least bit up on the bug situation across the big pond, they simply didn't hand out that many Exterminator of the Year awards to a rank amateur. Such a record speaks for itself, no matter the country of origin. *Translation:* The thought of being on the same team with Sir Delbert Prescott was a hell of a lot more comforting than with the previous pick.

"I'd be most honored to serve," the Brit said with a slight bow,"and am duly humbled by your confidence."

Gaven McCloud reached over and gave Prescott a good-natured pat on the shoulder.

"Goddamned foreigners taking away American jobs yet again," he said with a playful wink, to which the big Brit grinned a bit red-faced.

Pretty boy Garrison gestured towards the screen and it instantly faded back to a swirling, psychedelic blue.

"As for team member number three, let's just say the man's versatility speaks for itself."

He waived the same arm around as if gripping a magic wand, and I heard Beth groan. All the theatrics and stage drama antics were growing a bit thin on my nerves as well, and might well only serve as the sourest of memories for those not chosen to take the 'center stage'.

The screen re-lit, freeze-framing a trio of photos of the same individual posing in drastically different guises.

"Jesus crow," I heard Gaven McCloud spout, though I couldn't tell if the outburst was fueled by awe, disgust, or possibly a combination of both.

Photo one displayed an impossibly bulked-up, black-masked subject standing in the center of a fighting ring, his booted foot propped atop a middle rope while striking a body builder's pose. The man's biceps appeared as thick as my waist, while his neck, shoulders and chest appeared to have been welded together into one massive muscle growth. Can't say for sure the timeline for said snapshot, but

I'd be willing to wager a hefty sum it was before anyone caught distributing or ingesting any form of human growth hormone faced stiff felony charges.

Picture two was clearly that of an old Blu-Ray DVD film cover, the title and credits of which were conveniently blurred out. Despite the omissions, it was obvious this hadn't exactly been a Disney offering. The man stood at its center with his feet speed wide while two females, one African-American and the other Caucasian and both equally nude, bowed on either side of his massive thighs.

His groin area had, like the films title, been given the air brush treatment. Gotta say, it was one wide, lengthy blur at that. Never been a penis-envy kinda guy, you understand. Very comfortable in my manhood, in fact. Still, couldn't help but feel a slight twinge of inadequacy.

I heard Beth scoff, and could only hope she kept whatever smart-ass remark currently parked on her tongue planted firmly in cheek. In hindsight, I should've known better.

"Yeah, he *wishes*. Only if he was wearing a two-by-four strap-on," she mercifully whispered, though the volume knob had been turned up just enough to spur a muffled giggle from Gaven McCloud. Photo number three was apparently the most recent; a magazine or internet ad display featuring the man decked out in full exterminator regalia, his trademark sneer and thick, bared, heavily tattooed arms fully intact.

"Former East Coast Grappler's Heavyweight Wrestling Champion…while also infamous for the forty-six adult films in which he starred as 'Dick

Draper'- currently better known as the 'Ebony Assassin', I speak of course of Mister Luther Bohannon."

Now the shit was getting downright sickening. Self-congratulatory BS spewed forth from a company suit who no more cared about us than the thousands of slum-dwellers they'd booted from the area like so much stacked trash.

NAME: James Bohannon

KNOWN PROFESSIONALLY AS: 'The Ebony Assassin'

TITLE: Freelance Exterminator/security advisor/ bodyguard for-hire **AGE:** Unknown (presumed to be between thirty-five and thirty-eight) **SEX/RACE**: African-American Male

BORN: Tempe, Arizona

EXTERMINATOR SINCE: Undisclosed

MISC NOTE: Infamous as both former professional wrestler and internet porn star; retired from the former in two-thousand eleven and the latter in two-thousand thirteen.

ON THE PERSONAL SIDE: Unmarried, though internet buzz speculates once participated in a 'quickie Vegas marriage' to former blonde-goddess porn star *'Gallactica'*, a coupling that was swiftly dissolved. Rumored to charge upwards of two-thousand dollars an hour for his bodyguard services and at least twice that for home and business security issues.

P. C (Pest Control) CLAIM TO FAME: Has reportedly provided exterminator (as well as bodyguard and security advisor services) to some of

47

Hollywood's top movers and shakers, to include an A-list of actors, producers, and directors.

"Appreciate the intro, Mister Garrison, but let's just say I would've been shocked to hear otherwise," Bohannon croaked through a glittering, gold-tinted grille, his tree-trunk thick arms folded across a mostly bared, barrel-shaped chest.

Didn't really know how to take the man at the time, but there was a definite intimidation factor present. No way I was alone with such a vibe. The man had no doubt used that bull-horn voice and bulked-up physique to great advantage through the years. Beth gave no indication of her thoughts one way or another, though she was never one to let on in those rare occasions when someone frightened her by mere appearance alone.

As things were progressing, what with only three more candidates to be chosen for the 'team', I had a sinking feeling our partnership was going to be our undoing. After all, this was a numbers game, and unlike everyone else, Beth and I were taking up two slots.

Whirling on his heels, a bit too graceful for my taste-I was beginning to wonder if the 'Pretty Boy' part wasn't such a stretch after all-Garrison punched up the next image as his narration resumed in earnest.

"Since time is of great essence, let us cut to the chase and introduce team member number four…"

The grinning mug on display wasn't easily identified, that is until one read the grin as being born of pure smugness in lieu of natural amusement.

"Awwww, hell," Gaven McCloud quipped,"there goes the neighborhood."

NAME: Virgil Hobbs
KNOWN PROFESSIONALLY AS: 'The Cleaner'
TITLE: Founder/Owner of 'Annihilation' Pest Control chain
AGE: 37
SEX/RACE: African-American Male
BORN: Eerie, Indiana
EXTERMINATOR SINCE: March 2004, following a four-year stint in the U. S. Army (1999-2003)
MISC NOTES: Named Pennsylvania Exterminator of The Year (2008- 2009). 'Annihilation Pest Control' home office located in Philly, with smaller branches in Pittsburgh and Clayton, Penn. Despite business success, is legendary for his 'hands-on' approach to personalized service. Started career with 'Insecticide, Inc' out of Wichita Falls, Texas, sharing route time with Gaven McCloud, who has went on to found his own chain of stores in the Lone Star state.
ON THE PERSONAL SIDE: Married to Shonda for twelve years. Three children ages nine, seven, and four.
CLAIM TO FAME: Initially gained solid rep in the industry for fearless and unparalleled job performance while servicing some of lower Philly's most infamous metro housing developments. Following this, 'The Cleaner' also secured similar

49

contracts for Pittsburgh's deadly Ben J. Dove Projects, less-than-lovingly referred to by local police as 'Dodge City'.

To his credit, or perhaps it was just a natural dose of extraordinary cockiness, Virgil Hobb's lone response was a slight nod.

"Seriously, congrats Virg," Gaven McCloud said, leaning forward and shooting the other man a wink.

"Not necessary, Gaven," Hobbs responded, only briefly acknowledging the other man's gesture,"nothing complicated here. They need the best…now they've got 'im."

McCloud fell back in his chair and shrugged, the wry expression on his rugged face the definition of priceless.

"Yep. Proves my point exactly. Once a horses' ass, always a horses' ass."

"Welcome aboard, Mister Hobbs," Garrison said with yet another semi-bow, and I began to feel the faintest aching at the pit of my gut. Four down, two to go. What were the odds? Didn't exactly look promising for this kid or his gal Friday.

"And on to the next…it's always a kick to reacquaint old cohorts, I must say," he continued to prattle as the screen dimmed for a sec before reigniting with a new image, one that wasn't the least bit surprising, though the jolt of disappointment that accompanied it increased the discomfort at my midsection at least two-fold.

"Folks, let us meet team member number five, that being the pride of the Lone Star state, Gaven McCloud..."

"Now *there* truly goes the neighborhood..." Hobbs spat with little of the good humor of his former tech-mate, instead sounding more like a purposely smart-ass dis. The photo at hand was as comically exaggerated as I suspected was the man it showcased. Donning a ten-gallon Stetson, shiny black cowboy boots and a 'gun-belt' filled with various mini-flasks of pesticides in place of bullets, each of McCloud's gloved hands were poised over twin injector wands in lieu of actual firearms.

"Oh yeah," McCloud sighed in obvious relief, briefly clapping his hands in triumph,"that's what I'm talkin' about. You won't be sorry, Slick. As is my personal creed, I'll surely give ya all I got."

Grinning sheepishly, Pretty Boy Garrison's only response was a rather half-hearted 'thumbs up' gesture as McCloud's personal 'stat-sheet' materialized just beneath his photo.

NAME: Gaven McCloud

KNOWN PROFESSIONALY AS: 'The Texas Terminator'

TITLE: Founder/owner of 'Texas Terminators'; main office located in Arlington, Texas; additional branches in Houston, Paris, and Abilene, Texas.

AGE: Forty-one

SEX/RACE: Caucasian Male

BORN: Austin, Texas

51

EXTERMINATOR SINCE: Feb 2003, following six-year stint as a US Marine

MISC NOTES: Twice named finalist for Texas Exterminator of the Year, though was named runner-up on both occasions. Was employed by six different pest control companies from two-thousand three to two-thousand nine before going into business for himself.

ON THE PERSONAL SIDE: Thrice-divorced, currently single. Two children (son, 14; daughter, 11, from first wife)

CLAIM TO FAME: Received Medal of Honor due to heroic actions while serving in Iraqis Conflict. On March 11 of the year two-thousand two, then Corporal Gaven McCloud was credited with single-handedly rescuing three wounded members of his own unit, as well as an Iraqis family of four from a group of fanatical guerillas holding them hostage. Subsequently awarded a 'battlefield promotion' to Sergeant, McCloud concluded a fourteen month tour before returning home and being honorably discharged a few months later. He personally received his medal from President George W. Bush Jr. in an April eleven, two-thousand two ceremony held on the White House grounds.

Impressive-a bona-fide war hero to boot. Laid back, borderline clownish outer persona aside, there was definitely more to the Texas Terminator than meets the eye. Though it seemed an improbable long-shot at that point, I found myself wishing we could've called that man teammate, if just for a scant few days. As to further emphasize the ancient saw that 'you can't tell a book by its cover', McCloud pushed his chair back and stood rigidly, the old soldier in him evident in not only the pose, but the respectfully stern, matter-of-fact lilt to his overall tone.

"Appreciate the back-story congratulatory, Slick, but the war-story flashback wasn't at all necessary to the task at hand. Just a note to everyone present; ask me no questions and a war-story you'll never hear. What's past is past. Just wanted to spit that out right from the get-go, folks. Apologies, Slick…please continue. One more name to complete the set, I reckon."

Like I said, the man seemed to exhume class. A rare commodity in the business we all claimed as a career.

As to provide equal-time for McCloud's earlier nod, Virgil Hobbs leaned forward and addressed the man in a completely alien tone in terms of his *usual* verbal output. *Translation*; it was neither sarcastically mocking nor self- congratulatory.

"Hey Cloudy," he said, flashing a brief thumbs-up, "jarhead past aside, it's good to have you on board."

Not even bothering to meet the other man's gaze, McCloud's only response was a slight wink, no doubt some sort of subliminal signal between the two old comrades that would remain a mystery to all others present. There was definitely a history there, but one neither was going to be overly willing to share with relative strangers.

"Only fitting that we re-team Misters Hobbs and McCloud, as any familiarity in terms of the group could prove to be a true boon as the mission progresses," Garrison said, already priming his trigger thumb to reveal the last of the chosen.

"Alright good folks, we are down to revealing the final piece to the collective puzzle. Let me state this was not an easy task by any means or measure. All present have proven themselves as not only top-notch pest control techs but equally adapt business persons. There are no losers here, and I want to announce that those not chosen for what I like to refer to as the 'first team' are hereby invited to join our 'second team' as advisors. You will, of course, be well- compensated for any and all contributions you make to ensure mission success."

Damned if an immediate surge of adrenalin didn't cause my scared old ticker to pound like a revved-up jackhammer. Maybe the trip wouldn't be a colossal waste of time after all. Similarly, I saw Beth's ashen-pale cheeks rosey-up, telling me all I needed to know in terms of what she saw our chances as.

Basically, slim and none, and Slim had done high-stepped out of the conference room with his butt-cheeks ablaze.

"Please don't interpret this offer as anything resembling pity," Garrison continued, arching an eyebrow,"believe me when I say the corporation is beyond such trivial emotion when it comes to matters of big business."

No possibility of a fib there. At least he'd found the decency to spout at least one solid truth in-between well-rehearsed spiels. Who cares how obvious the statement, I'm sure we all appreciated a little honesty amid the mounds of bull.

"We need all the valuable input we can get here, folks, and you're the best in the business. Now, without further ado," he chimed, sliding gracefully (again, too damn graceful for my taste-a veritable 'twinkle toes' he was) to the left just as the screen reignited one last time,"here is team member number six, plus one…"

Downright weird as it may sound, for a single split-second I truly didn't recognize either of the mug-shots on display. Maybe it was the shock-the unexpected jolt of staring straight into a pair of partially bloodshot orbs that belonged to yours truly that triggered the temporary amnesia. Truthfully, it was the image of Beth's familiar half-smile, half-grimace that snapped me back into a semblance of reality, though not before I'd noticed each of my fingers had gone numb to the knuckles in the process.

"We fully understand the internal financial ramifications of such a technical snafu, that being we've settled on seven team members instead of the planned six, but logically there was simply no way to split up such a proven partnership without instigating a negative ripple effect amongst the ranks. In other words, all seven chosen individuals will receive a full share, as originally stated. So, without further ado, let us check those vital statistics…"

NAME(S): Jack Barton & Beth Cambridge

KNOWN PROFESSIONALLY AS: 'J & B'

TITLE: Founders, owner/operators of 'Bug-Stompers Incorporated', focusing on freelance pest control assignments to include government and state contracted jobs. Main office located in Richmond, Virginia; additional branch located in Blacksburg.

AGES: Jack: Thirty-nine. Beth: Thirty-six.

SEX/RACE: Jack: Caucasian male. Beth: Caucasian female.

BORN: Jack: Louisville, Kentucky. Beth: Myrtle Beach, South Carolina.

EXMINATOR(S) SINCE: Jack: January 2000. Beth: July 2003.

MISC NOTES: Both worked at various pest control companies, eventually opening their first business (J & B's Pest Eliminators) in March 2009.

Renamed 'Bug Stompers Incorporated' in September of 2011, they specialized in taking on state and city contracts other companies wouldn't touch, including servicing project housing in such urban war-zones as Cleveland's infamous 'gangland' district and Chicago's Latino slums, nicknamed the 'Tortilla Flats'.

ON THE PERSONAL SIDE: Though rumored to have once been linked romantically, each currently describes their relationship as strictly professional. Subordinates have nicknamed them the 'Sonny & Cher' of the pest control business, referencing a popular 20th Century pop-culture couple.

ClAIM(S) TO FAME: The afore-mentioned, well-publicized extermination of the infamous, ultra-violent 'Tortilla Flats' section of Chicago

Public Housing, a harrowing, three-week stint that saw Jack, Beth and three of their hired guns spray, bait, retreat, fog and *re*-retreat a total of one-thousand, six-hundred and nineteen units infested with everything from German cockroaches to millipedes to Black Widow spiders. Labeled 'mission improbable' by none other than the city mayor himself (who was at the time pushing a bill to demolish the projects and use the expansive area to erect office buildings for new downtown businesses), Jack, Beth and their team worked anywhere from fourteen to sixteen hour shifts for the mission's duration until the multiple infestations were officially listed as 'under control' by the state health department. Rumor (supposedly spread by one of the 'hired' guns) had it that the group used over three-thousand ounces of pesticide mix per day on the sites, translating roughly to thirty- six gallons per day, along with upwards of seven-hundred grams of gel baits and an unknown amount of miscellaneous can and injector sprays.

As a postscript, Jack and Beth received numerous 'special' citations from Hispanic community leaders, who called their efforts 'Herculean' and the end results nothing short of miraculous. Miracle or not, the performance also won the team a permanent, not to mention substantially lucrative, monthly contract servicing the projects.

"Foul! I for one cry *foul,* damn it!" Brad Bedford shrieked just as I was about to offer my official thanks. I had spent less than an hour in

'Killer Bee's' less than charming presence, but had already awarded him the title of 'most annoying', low praise indeed considering such heady, egotistical competition.

Jolted by Bedford's warbling screech, Garrison fell out of character just long enough to perform a comical two-step, no doubt a common reaction for his ilk at being so rudely barked at. Ah, blood will tell, most notably when the lower- middle and upper classes clash.

"Mister Bedford, you shouldn't take this as being shunned. As I've stated, the remainder of you are indeed welcome to join the team as well-compensated advis-..."

Red-faced and ranting, I swear Bedford's grade-school tantrum switched effortlessly into second gear; his high-pitched caterwauling reaching glass- shattering proportions.

"Fuck that noise, Vest. I don't need corporate charity. This boy came here expecting first-rate treatment, not banishment to some...*second level* bullshit status. I'm Killer-Bee Bedford, man, the best damn bug assassin you'll ever have the honor of sharing space with. I'm either startin', or I'm departin', got it?"

"Exit door's right behind ya, Ace," McCloud said, pointing a thumb towards the exit.

"Just in case your waitin' on somebody to beg you to stay...don't strain those youthful lungs holdin' your breath."

Swear to god, I almost clapped. Beth echoed similar thoughts later that night.

True to his infantile nature, Bedford stood while tossing the chair aside,

shot a double-barreled bird Garrison's way before pausing at the exit for dramatic effect.

"Can't say about the rest of the 'rejects', but I'll be rooting for the bugs to chew your collective asses to oatmeal."

"Better get back to Daycare, Junior," Virgil Hobbs snapped without bothering to turn around, "this here mission is for adults only."

Bedford huffed, giving the doorframe a solid whack upon departure.

Giving his forehead a playful slap, 'Terminator' Bohannon shocked the masses with a completely off-the-wall attempt at backhanded humor, a trait I was unaware the 'human wall' was even capable of. Then again, I'd surmise a person would have to possess a certain degree of 'court jester' levity in order to make a living as a porn star.

"Damn shame losing that one. Sure would've been a comfort having him watch my back. Arrogant little shit sounded more like a soggy *gnat* than a killer bee." Even Garrison's tight-ass posture relaxed a bit at that, and we quickly got back down to business, the first order of which was a briefly delayed acceptance speech.

"Appreciate the opportunity, Mister Garrison," I croaked a bit louder than originally anticipated and unable to completely shake the nervous edge from my voice.

"Ditto, buddy-boy," Beth injected with an icy-cool sliver of calm collectiveness I'd always envied,"you and the other pressed suits won't be

59

sorry." If anything affected that woman in terms of shaking her self-confidence, I'd yet to witness it.

Peering back and forth from Beth to myself and back again, Garrison's pasted-on grin reset itself with frightening ease.

"No problem, you two. We were…forced to bend our rules a bit to expand the roster, but there is indeed a method to our madness."

Positive vibes aside, I quickly reminded myself to trust no one save Beth. This was no Tinsel-Town awards banquet after all. There were two distinct sides represented here: those who came for the money and those who were to dole it out. The former were to ply their specialized trade to the latter, who had a big problem to solve and were damned desperate to solve it. Cut and dry, plain and simple. It would never be about pats on the back. It was strictly business from both sides, each of which had a hell of a lot to lose if things went sour. We weren't just talking financial loss either, but loss of life itself.

"Alright then," Garrison concluded, the relief evident in the sudden weariness of his tone,"the roster is set. The chosen team will now be shuttled to their hotel for room assignments and a fine meal, all courtesy of New Horizons.

As for the four still present that weren't chosen, please come up and see me now concerning further assignment."

Quick as that, we were loaded into a waiting hydro-van and whisked off to the downtown Hyatt Regency Supreme (upwards of three-hundred bucks a night per room, rumor had it), where everyone was given key-cards to luxury suites that I could only speculate as being some of the most expensive in the building. Before sacking out, we were indeed fed from a surprisingly expansive menu from the hotel restaurant before being handed printed itineraries. Funny, but no one had a lot to say during the meal or afterwards as we scurried off to our individual rooms. Not surprising really, considering what lay ahead. Guess it was decided by silent proxy that future opportunities for such peace and quiet might well be few and far between. Personally, I was pretty damn wiped from both the trip and all the dramatics from that day's initial meeting. Beth's sagging eyelids and drooping shoulders spoke volumes to her overall state of being, and even Gaven McCloud had discovered an inner 'mute' button while inhabiting a booth all to his lonesome.

Covering myself with cool, satin sheets within my spacious single room's ultra-comfy climes, I scanned the list between clicking channels on the blue-ray plasma taking up the entirety of a nearby wall. Starting at six AM the very next morning, things were apt to get interesting to the point of being downright spicy. Seriously, I would've expected nothing less.

BUG OUT, PART FOUR

War Stories at Ground Zero

The next morning saw a considerable loosening of tongues among the troops, quite possibly spurred by either a good night's shuteye or an overall vibe that the mission ahead wasn't near as treacherous as predicted by those signing the paychecks. Though I did feel somewhat recharged, my own personal vibe, that of a heavily cloaked foreboding you could slice with a butter knife, hadn't shifted nary an inch. Chalk it up to the seven-plus hours of peaceful snoozing then. Either way, as we sat around the dining table inhaling buttermilk biscuits, crispy bacon with freshly scrambled eggs and the finest in gourmet java's, spirits seemed high as the flow of banter was dosed out in equal measure.

No matter the occupation of men, there is always present a level of unadulterated BS in terms of past accomplishments and/or conquests. To say the least, Pest Control is no exception, especially considering the dramatic alternation in subterranean enemies over the previous decade. In the forty-five minutes to an hour the group spent nibbling and sipping before the issue of getting down to the job at hand interrupted, it seemed each had a story to share.

In a nutshell, passed on in true 'Readers Digest' condensed format, are samples that were tossed out for individual consumption. For all the World, the scene reminded me of the classic twentieth century Spielberg flick, 'Jaws', wherein a trio of shark hunters exchanged tales while comparing battle scars.

Of the half-dozen war stories to spew forth (only Commander Virgil passed, surprising considering the man's legendary ego), some of which were mercifully brief-Bohannon battling a Black Recluse infestation in the home of a former big-time Hollywood producer; Prescott's two-day skirmish with a nesting of skin-bore ants at the secluded ranch of a former member of British Parliament, two easily stood out from the rest. One for its exaggerated, outlandish, borderline Sci-Fi claims, and the second for the element of stark terror involved. As for Bug-Stomper's Incorporated, I allowed Beth to choose a specific incident from our sordid past and run with it in her own unique style. Not only did I claim no skills as a storyteller, my long-term memory was weak at best. I always had been a 'live in the present' type.

Instead of the expected half-hour rant, Beth kept it surprisingly short and concise, and with very little in any in the way of dramatics (i. e. , her usual eye- rolling, hand-gesturing hysterics). It had been the early spring of two-thousand twelve, the ink barely dry on a deal that would have us treat over sixteen-hundred apartments in Chicago's infamous eastside slums known regionally as the 'Tortilla Flats'. According to the Metro Housing officials we'd spoken to, nine companies had attempted to successfully treat the units over a four year span, all eventually breaching contract for various reasons, the most prominent being potentially bodily harm to company employees, along with the resignation that the monthly treatments were 'doing little' to alleviate the multiple infestations on site. A year earlier, Beth and I had taken on the Gangland district in Cleveland and were eventually awarded a city citation for enacting 'superior control measures'. It wasn't as if we hadn't waded ankle deep in project filth before and dealt with it as only true professionals can. Though there's always a measure of apprehension when taking on such a monumental, seemingly impossible task, once a price is set, the contracts are signed and the obligation becomes reality, Beth and I always treat each and every job the same regardless of scope; failure simply isn't a viable option. May sound corny, but up until that point the constant obsessing coupled with a slightly arrogant, 'can-do' attitude had worked wonders in putting Bug-Stomper's inc on the map. Long story short, the three weeks spent treating, re-treating, fogging and cleaning up the Flats was without a doubt the longest of my life; an excruciating, bug-eradicating marathon that saw six tech's (counting Bethy and myself) pull shifts ranging anywhere from fourteen to seventeen hours.

In-between we endured abuse both verbal and physical (I was actually gut-punched by a doped-up, three-hundred-plus pound Hispanic male who'd mistaken me for a member of the A. T. F whom he'd presumed was raiding his unit). Similarly, one of our techs (Kevin *Dirty Harry* Callahan, a former Detroit cop and Private Eye) had his left eye practically gouged out by some paranoid, crank-headed chick who'd jumped out of a closet, where she'd been hiding from a vengeful pimp. Hardships aside, and there were a butt-load, treatments were completed on schedule and with better-than-average results, earning us not only a hefty bonus but also several community service awards from local leaders.

Little did we know at the time, but we'd been the Flats last chance, as the city council had already voted for mass evictions and demolition if our efforts had failed. As it was, our bi-monthly sprayings kept the place afloat until newer units were constructed at a separate location, thereby saving almost three-thousand tenants from forced homelessness. Heroes, one might suggest? Nah, just a small pest control company building its rep the only way it knew how, by working hard and providing a quality service in even the most extreme of cases. While telling the tale, Beth's subdued tone and calm demeanor had done me proud. It wasn't like her to low-key such a potentially bravado-filled slice of our glorious history-a one-hundred eighty degree turn from the boisterous, over-the-top personality I'd grown so accustomed to tolerating. Whatever her reason, it impressed me no end.

Now to the cream of the crop, starting (logically) at the beginning:

It wasn't exactly a shock that the whole shebang was unofficially kicked-off by Doc Braggs, his last name truly fitting for one so obviously enamored with one's self.

The good Doc stated (though certainly not in verbatim; again, this boy's memory has never been *that* sharp) in between noisy slurps of a steaming, pitch- black Columbian brew:

"It all transpired back in the summer of two-thousand seven—I'm talking late July or early August and smack-dab in the middle of the Arizona desert no less.

Hot enough to melt your gonads to your thigh, man. The good doctor was barely in residency at that time—green as fresh puke and just learning the trade, you understand. Talk about wet behind the ears... this boy was wearing the virgin bug-killer label like a shiny neon sign. Anyhow, the second-rate company that gave me my humble start had contracted a two-day 'treat and beat' out in the middle of the desert at some long-closed Mexican buffet joint that was prepping for a grand re-opening. Talk about the middle of nowhere, this place was off the severely beaten path, man. Twenty miles from the nearest town and ten more from the closest interstate ramp.

I shit you not, the three of us appointed the task of cleaning that ultra-nasty burrito box weren't just greeted by your everyday nest of cock-a-roaches, no senor. When I say the greasy little son's of bitches were literally holding the place up, it ain't far from the god's honest truth. Not just your everyday SS variety either, but American, Peruvian, and Jamaican skin-peelers tossed in for good measure. A ver-i-table melting pot of roach stew, the actual population of which might've ranged in the billions, though it was impossible to accurately gauge. Well, we fogged that two-story bug-stand a grand total of eleven times over the next seventy-two hours; sucking dry around twenty gallons of Demon Elite in the process. No exaggeration, man, if you stood in one place too long, there stood the realistic danger of being shuffled about like a mall mannequin if enough of the little boogers wedged their way under your chem boots. I know, I know...we've all seen our share of swarms, but this was different. This was literally of the ocean-waves variety. It was around noon of day three's fumigating party that we discovered the true source of the swarms, though purely by accident. Started out innocently enough...one of the senior techies fell thigh- deep through a rotted plank and in the process of pulling him out and brushing his suit free of scuttling varmints, it turned out the building had a sealed-over basement that someone had gone to great pains to keep hidden. Once a few more boards had been pulled free, a trio of us were handpicked to suit up, load up, and buck up for a ride into the dark unknown. Sounds cornball I know, but man...it really felt like we were being lowered into a pocket of outer space not meant for human habitation. The boss had rigged up a pretty damned ingenious robe 'n crane contraption, and one by one the three of us were dropped into the abyss. Maybe ten to twelve feet in, the first thing that hit me...and thump me like a fifty-pound sledge it did...was the smell. Found myself gagging into my mask, despite having loaded in new filters just prior to entry. Can't really describe it without dredging up the memory...hell, my eyes are beginning to pool just thinking about it, but needless to say, it put the 'rot' in rotten. Didn't take long to locate the source once our boots hit solid ground...or maybe I should say 'mushy' ground, 'cause damned if we hadn't been lowered smack-dab in the middle of the feeding frenzy to end all such frenzies. I'm talking mountains of maggots versus armies of roaches in the grisliest damn all-you-can-eat buffet you could imagine. Once my flashlight froze onto a few well-lit images, I felt my gut commence to churn and turn at warp speed, and was afraid I was about to fill my mask with the remains of that morning's continental breakfast. Needless to say, we didn't stick around to join in on the fun as possible desert trays, the three of us screamin' like spooked girl-scouts to be hauled the hell out of that nauseating pit.

Once we all managed a lungful of semi-fresh air and were able to explain what we'd seen to the site boss, he got on the horn and called the local fuzz, who in turn dialed up the state authorities for a look-see, along with a full-blown Hazmat team.

All told, they dug up parts of forty-one bodies from that damn meat pit, most of 'em in the latter stages of decomp but a few the local coroner later claimed were no more than a week or so old. State officials later confirmed that the place had been used by some local chapters of the Mexican Mafia as a dump site for those who'd been opposing their takeover of the Phoenix/Tempe area.

Once the harvest of corpses was complete, we were allowed back in to finish the job we'd been contracted to do. Can't say I was exactly thrilled to re-enter that damn slaughterhouse, but hey, cash is cash, you dig?

Looking back, it's a damn wonder a black cloud of that toxic shit didn't form over her roof from the desert sky, only to piss pesticide on the patrons at a later date. In the aftermath, I guarantee we vacc'd up at least a hundred pounds worth of husks. I know for a fact I emptied that damn bug-bag a good fifty times in-between suck-up sessions. As for the two dudes that assisted in that monumental cleaning, I never heard from either of 'em again once we returned to the shop. Guess they decided they'd seen enough bug carcasses to last a lifetime. You guys know the business; biggest damn revolving door of new employees this side of the prison guard trade.

As for the Taco Palace or whatever it was renamed, I've heard since it closed down after a six or seven month run and finally got put out of its misery by the state health board via a bulldozer's blade. Good friggin' riddance I say, though to this day no exterminator alive can claim losing his cherry in such a dramatic fashion. Well, that's the story, folks. Believe it...nor not."

Next came Gaven McCloud, who had temporarily halted his furious assault on a pile of buttermilk biscuits to regale us with easily (at least to me) the most harrowing story of all. Though it was lengthy, at least a half-hour in duration, there wasn't a single dull moment nor attempted interruption from anyone present as to shorten the tale. All in all, it was campfire material alright, though definitely for adult ears only.

"Good one, kid. Color me impressed, seeing as I lost my own roach- croaking virginity in a series of middle and upper--class homes outside of Arlington. Now, allow me to lay a real knee-shaker

69

on ya. Unlike the doc's isolated spic eatery, this particular incident is more of what ya might call an urban nightmare, downtown Dallas style.

Also unlike the good doctor, I recall names, dates and times in crystal clear clarity, though I sincerely wish that weren't the case. Fact is, I'd love nothin' better than to brain-fart the whole ugly mess away for the duration. Date was November sixteen of the year two-thousand six. Me and three other techies arrived on site at exactly six-thirteen PM. A very rare flare-up of snow flurries had hit the twin cities, that being Dallas/Fort Worth, earlier that day and was still coating the pavement. I recall the four of us feelin' mighty pissed at bein' called out to treat a full two hours after our official shift had ended. Naturally we were all salaried, so pullin' OT of any form or fashion was a moot point in terms of financial gain. Thinkin' back, its pretty evident that our lazy, double-dealin' branch manager knew exactly what he was doin' by stayin' clear of the area and sendin' out a few cronies instead, two of which were as green as fresh-picked spinach on the job and thereby expendable in his eyes. Like I said, grade-A horse's anus, and then some. In fact, over the years I've based everything I do and say as a supervisor by doing the exact opposite of that selfish prick. Ya might say he was a reverse roll-model of sorts.

Anyhow, the site in question wasn't really anything out of the ordinary. The company had tons of commercial contracts in what was referred to as the 'Shoe-Horn' district on the far eastern edge of the big-D city limits. The area mostly consisted of industrial warehouses and the like, some of which seemed to change ownership on a bi-monthly basis. Well, this particular job called for the mass spraying and bating of a former sports complex turned live concert venue whose new owners were kickin' off the holiday season a few short weeks with some kinda Christmas-themed opera show. Bein' that the place held ten- thousand-plus seats and was damned near twenty-thousand square feet, we all knew this wasn't gonna be your typical half-hour to forty-five minute hose-down. We were lookin' at two hours at the very least, even with four bodies splitting the duty. I think what peeved us the most was the timing. I mean, why a nighttime spraying? Being that the place was 'closed for renovations' anyhow, why not eight AM, noon or at the very least a three PM set-time? I mean, we all know they're more active after sunset, but it wasn't like we had to see the scurrying little bastards in order to treat 'em. I figured it was simply a case of our bone-headed boss kissin' client ass once again. Whatever the reason, we were all screwed and damned well knew it (laughed). Strolling into that joint like a gang of pissed off Brahma bulls with flarin', smokin' nostrils, the four of us were hauling boulder-sized bricks on our shoulders, each of us bitchin' and cussin' at the conniving bozo responsible for our being sent there after 'regular' duty hours. I can only speculate that the group rage thing we had goin' kinda blinded us from a common sense standpoint. More on that later. I myself was in-between wives and had been datin' this hot little number outta Arlington who'd promised me various

71

carnal pleasures that particular evening-needless to say I was less than thrilled with the prospect of missin' out. Lord, talk about what you think are big problems shrinking in comparison, by the time that night's festivities came to a merciful close, I swear I couldn't even think of that girl's full name.

Myself and a vet Tech named Wilt Jenkins, a one-time Marine nicknamed 'Kong' for his shovel-sized mitts and size sixteen feet, had been assigned to hose down the upper deck seating while the other two dudes, Joe 'Blockhead' Braxton and Lomax 'The Hawk' Hornsby, were to treat the lower. Ol' Kong was a hoot; big Louisiana lummox with a heart as big as all outdoors. Always loved workin' with the man, since he was one of the few techies I'd known whose secondary language wasn't of the constant 'bitch and moan ' variety. Kong generally took things in stride no matter the level of personal inconvenience.

Now, back to the issue of common sense, as in: one or more of us really should'a figured something was mighty fishy that the joint had been unlocked upon entry, being that the client was nowhere in site. I mean, Hell's Belles, we weren't exactly talkin' about the safest neighborhood in D-Town by any stretch, as some of the city's roughest projects was less than a stone's throw away. It was damned obvious none of us were exactly thinkin' straight, the main focus bein' hose the place down and vamoose as soon as humanly possible.

Personally, I recall marching at a 'double-time' pace between those narrowly- spaced seats while keeping a constant spray at ankle level. Not to be outdone,"Kong' Jenkins was practically sprinting his way through. Married with six or seven kids, old shovel-mitts was likely frettin' about the beat-down his old lady was apt to apply for her loving bread-winner showing up two hours late.

I'd say we'd covered approximately half the upper deck in less than twenty minutes when the first scream stopped us both dead in our tracks, my own clumsy skid almost sending me sailing over the short-porch railing. Jenkins and I exchanged wide-eyed glances without makin' a sound, as if waitin' for a follow-up wail in order to officially confirm we'd heard the first. Well, it didn't take long, Amigo. Wasn't ten ticks before the dead air of that dimly lit coliseum was filled with a banshee-howl of historical proportions. I'm talkin' a man with his gonads firmly ensnared in a bear trap type cry. Painful as it is to confess, that was the closest this grown man had ever come to whizzin' in his Dickies. Leastwise, 'til about five minutes later, when said floodgates weren't quite as successful in holdin' back the yellow-tinted waters.

"Wh-what the fuck Cloudy?" Kong had asked with a dramatic tilt of his buzz-cut shaved, oversized and slightly warped noggin. Man, try as I might, I'll never forget that look.

"Probably just Blockhead messin' with our heads, man," I'd answered, tryin' like hell to keep my throat from clicking like a spooked rooster in the process. Now, its one thing to buy your own BS on some primeval level...altogether another in understanding it's a steaming pile of excrement the second it escapes one's own tremblin' lips.

73

"Yeah, th-that's it," Jenkins had babbled in response, all shakin' and wide- eyed, lookin' all the world like a spooked six-grader on the verge of spewin' a chocolate malted into his drawers. Kong stood six-four if he was an inch, with the barrel chest and broad shoulders of a lifelong gym rat, and just witnessing the big lummox's meltdown unnerved me no end. I mean, shit, the guy was a war vet, after all.

"Calm down, Kong...you're givin' me the willies."

Well-worn clichés aside, in those next few seconds a pin-droppin' on that hardwood flooring would've been the equivalent of an M-80 detonation. I mean, it was creepy-quiet.

Me and Kong crept over to that balcony's railed deck like a pair of heavily medicated slugs, no doubt resemblin' the same type bug we'd been hired to exterminate. Well, we were so locked into scannin' the lower deck with its newly constructed stadium seating and curtained stage that we never heard nor caught a glimpse of the dude sneakin' up behind us.

"Hey, bug men," the stranger whispered, pausing just long enough between words to cock the handgun he no doubt was aiming our way, *"drop the juice-wands and follow me."*

Can't speak for Kong, but not once did I allow myself even the slightest glance towards the face of the man holding us at gunpoint, even as we walked past 'im and were led to floor level via a side stairwell. I did note his tall, lanky frame, and from the casual, cocky delivery and street savvy edge in

74

his voice, I'd have guessed black male, early to mid-twenties.

Long story a bit shorter, the four of us had stumbled blind as a pack of mules into some kinda extortion scenario gone as sour as a quart of whole milk with a month-old expiration date. Textbook case of wrong damn place, wrong damn time, only on a major scale whose ending clearly read 'tragic consequences'.

Kong and me were herded back stage behind the still-pulled curtain and introduced to a pair of self-proclaimed street bulls named 'Killa Z' and 'Thunder T', each of whom specialized in high-interest loans of the 'pay or be clay' variety. Z was a stick-thin black dude with a shaved, football-shaped head and a mouth full'a gold that sparkled like lit coals even in the semi-darkness. The loud-mouth little shit, whose entire vocabulary seemed to revolve around the words 'mother-fucker' might've been as old as thirty or as young as eighteen...it was near impossible to gauge from either his profanity-laced rants or constant, comical arm-wavin' antics. A loony-tunes cartoon character straight from the BET channel, the 'Killas' exact opposite in both size and demeanor was 'Thunder T'. Sporting a foot-high afro and with a physique borrowed from Jabba-The-Hut, the big man's soft-spoken, downright eloquent verbalizations were as ominous and bone-chillin' scary as his partners were unintentionally hilarious.

"Looks like this just isn't your night, boys," he'd said, wringin' his chubby hands together as if

attemptin' to strike up a flame from the building friction.

"Not really your fault, but that certainly doesn't change the facts, now does it?"

"Fuckin' A, Tee," Killa added, hoppin' about like a crank-addicted jackrabbit,"ya gonna dice 'em, Tee? Ya gonna gut their cracker asses just like those other two?"

Thunder Tee didn't bother a verbal response, continuin' to stare us both down while shakin' his head from side to side. It was around that time that I noticed an overturned B&G layin' at the edge of the stage. The letters B-HEAD were written in dark magic marker down its silver outer layer, along with a slew of blood spatters. Told me all I wanted to know about ol' Blockhead's fate, though if I were to guess I'd have said the screams had belonged to Hawk. Either way, things were lookin' pretty damn bleak for the home team.

"How's about lettin' me shank 'em, Tee? Shiiieeeet, I ain't carved me no white meat in weeks."

Mercifully, there ain't many instances in a man's life where his heart flat out stops beating as if somebody had reached inside and unplugged all the major arteries like a cruel practical joke, only to shove 'em back into place a few ticks later. Well, for yours truly, this was far from a virgin experience. I'd seen many a good man die in Iraq, and come damn near bitin' the bullet myself on several occasions. Then again, that was war. By comparison, there was no honor in bein' spoken of like so much processed lunchmeat. I heard Kong release a low, squeaky fart beside me, no doubt the big man's equivalent, however crude, to tossin' in the white flag. There was suddenly no doubtin' the validity of the screams we'd heard, nor the unfortunate originators. Blockhead and The Hawk were down for the count, most likely skewered in some grisly gangland manner, while our mystery client for the evening had yet to make even a token appearance. I had a feelin' we weren't fated to make the man's acquaintance, at least not within normal perimeters such as all involved still owned a working pair of lungs or with all fingers and toes intact. Dudes name had been typed on our invoice, but damned if I recalled it 'til 'Killa Z' blurted it out in-between death threats. Jerome Sanders, recent proprietor of the yet-to-be christened 'Silk Vibes' Entertainment Center, formerly the 'Horn Sports Complex'. It was later revealed that Sanders had hoped to spotlight up and coming hip-hop acts, along with the occasional 'memory lane' R&B acts of old. Problem was, he'd made two fatal miscalculations in purchasin' the place.

Number one with a bullet, so to speak, was acquirin' a business loan from a pair of grille-toothed sharks named Kajue 'Killa Z' Wilkes and Tony 'Thunder Tee' Thomason. Seems Sanders had agreed to certain conditions of the loan, to include booking whatever wanna-be rapper kin or posse member Wilkes and Thomason suggested. Instead, Sanders had rejected the idea after the fact, ignoring each request and essentially flashin' his 'loan officers' a big, fat middle finger.

Number two, and equally as hazardous if not more so, this Sanders bozo had become sadly delinquent in his payments. Rumor had it he'd even been so bold as to secure a second loan from a mysterious donor said to be a bitter rival of misters Wilkes and Thomason. Seems pretty obvious that Jerome Sanders wasn't exactly law school material, right? Little wonder the four of us strolled in without warnin' into a street-style slaughterhouse. Bad timing ain't the word...this was downright tragic.

"L-listen guys," Kong said, raisin' both of his dozer-blade sized mitts into the air while whimperin' like a spooked ankle-biter wakin' from a particularly nasty nightmare.

"We...ain't gonna...we ain't gonna say anything 'bout what...what's gone down h-here. Not a word, right C-Cloudy?"

I recall thinkin' for a minute the man was actually gonna say 'scout's honor' at some point in his beggin' rant.

"Um...Yeah, yeah...that's right," I babbled, my throat feelin' so parched it was like I'd just swallowed a quart of lighter fluid,"far as I'm concerned, we never arrived here this night. Got...got lost on the way. None of us know this area of town, ya know. Wouldn't be hard to get turned arou-..."

With the hoisting of a single finger against his oversized lips, the Killa stopped my ramblin' dialogue in its tracks.

"You guys sure there ain't a posse of back-up exterminators on the way as we rap?" he asked,

78

flashin' those shiny choppers yet again while pacin' between us and his mammoth sidekick, "you know, bug-mashin' reinforcements and all that shit?"

By this time, Kong's hands were flesh-covered windmills rotatin' about in a 'wax-on, wax-off' motion.

"N-no...we, that is...the four of us was it. Two men per truck. There ain't nobody else." After a two to three tick pause, durin' which time I could've hopped in and backed Kong's story but didn't on account of the red-hot bile filin' my throat, Thunder Tee finally chimed in.

"I don't know, fellas. These are some seriously spacious digs for just four dudes to hose."

He turned towards Killa, who snapped too like somebody had stuck a pig-sticker up between his narrow ass-cheeks.

"Better post two of the crew at the entrance...just in case somebody here isn't being completed honest."

"I'm on it, Tee."

The little runt practically genuflected before stormin' off to obey orders, leavin' little doubt of who was King Thug between the two.

As Kong resumed his 'lets make a deal' plea, even fallin' onto one knee for desired pathetic appeal, I couldn't help but take note that the present ranks of the hostage takers had been reduced to just two in wake of Killa and the others swift departure. It was also about that same time I took a quick self-inventory by allowing each of my hands to slide towards my chemical belt and the three attached mini-holsters located at the pit of my back.

Don't get me wrong-this boy ain't the hero-type, far from it, but there was little doubtin' the fact that me and Kong weren't apt to walk away from the situation in the best of health. In other words, we were dead meat on a stick as things stood, so why not give stayin' alive a chance, no matter how downright ludicrous the attempt. As the old sayin' went, desperate times call for desperate measures, and brother, we weren't just talkin' your run of the mill desperation here. It wasn't A-ball or even Triple-A...it was the show, the Major Leagues, man...life or death type shit that wasn't gonna be decided in days or hours, but minutes. Whatever I was gonna try, it had to be soon. As for my buddy Kong, the threat of immanent death had transformed 'im into a quiverin' six-foot-four pile of Banana Pudding. Wasn't sure how much help he'd be in a pinch while in such a state, but it wasn't about to stop me from proceedin' on with the plan, pathetic as she was.

"Guess if it weren't for bad luck, you boys wouldn't have no luck at all," said Thunder Tee in a soft whisper, the giggle that followed pissin' me off far worse than the heavy dose of sarcasm. Just the thought of this bloated Godfather wanna-be demeanin' us like we rated far below his murderin', thievin' ass turned all my fear into a pure, tangible rage. Meanwhile, Kong resumed his feeble pleas-beggin' a worthless thug half his age to spare his life.

"C-Cloudy and m-me...we're not gonna say a word. You gotta believe m- me, mister...um...mister

Tee. We...I mean, we just ain't the snitch type, you know?"

Saddest damn thing I've ever seen, really, to this very day. Personally, I've got more respect for an overstuffed crap-beetle than the piece of human garbage that dared threaten our lives over some third-party loan-shark deal gone south. As seconds passed and Kong's jabberin' dialogue began to slow, I came to the conclusion that if nothin' else, the man's incessant mumblin' might serve as just the right diversion. I only knew one thing for sure-if I was gonna act, it had to be before 'Killa' and his cronies returned to restack the odds for the bad guys. I sucked in a deep, silent breath while reachin' back with tinglin' fingers towards the trio of holsters.

"A man will say anything to save his own hide, Mister Exterminator," Thunder Tee replied, turnin' that cruiser-liner sized bulk of his about in slow-motion as to face away from us.

"Cruel as it may seem, I'm afraid we cannot afford to leave any loose-ends dangling, you understand. My apologies, gentlemen, but it is, after all, just business."

I watched old lard-butt's lone remainin' bodyguard shuffle towards' im as the two closed ranks for a whisper session, no doubt to discuss the quickest means of extermination, if you'll pardon the expression.

With both palms filled, I positioning my trigger fingers before slowly movin' my arms forward like some doped-up gunslinger. Talk about your flashbacks-for a second I was back in the desert.

Only wish I'd been toting my trusty M-16 instead of bug-bait. Regardless, nervous ain't a strong enough word for the ailment overtakin' me as I lunged forth. . Scared barely scratches the surface. In the end, it was all about adrenaline. I could've gone the Kong way of snivelin' coward suckin' his oversized thumb to the very end, or I could do my damndest to save our hides. From an outsider's point of view, it wasn't much of a contest in terms of matchin' firepower. The bodyguard was toting a nine mil, Glock if I was to guess, while King Thunder Thighs had either a forty-four or forty-five tucked inside his triple-X sized waistband. As for the home team, I was strapped with nothin' less than two tubes of Dupont's finest Demon-X liquid gels, the label of which warned explicably against contact with human flesh. They weren't just bluffin' neither, as most of ya probably know. I accidentally dribbled a pea-sized bead of that acidic crap on my bare forearm a few years back and watched my skin peel away like I'd dipped it in a vat of toxic waste. As for a game plan, I wasn't just aimin' for skin, per say, but directly for the peepers.

I heard Kong gasp soon as I lurched forward in the direction of the hired gun, aimin' my right fist and pressin' the back end of that tubes plastic plunger with every ounce of energy my tremblin' thumb could muster. Gotta say I got more outta Kong than I could've ever hoped as far as assistance goes. I'd already written the big fella off as a powder-puff who'd been permanently castrated once the screamin' had started.

82

Now, I could sit here, lie my ever-lovin' ass off and tell you folks one helluva 'big fish that got away' story. You know, how I single-handedly wiped out the whole heavily-armed gang with nothin' more than a pair of four-ounce tubes of Demon-X gel and these two fists, but I'm afraid the inner-conscience simply won't allow such unmediated bullshit to spew forth. Truth is, the facts I'm about to lay out are essentially word for word when compared to the statement given to Dallas-Metro's finest later that very night as yours truly was laid out on a hospital gurney and bein' loaded into an ambulance. It ain't like every minute detail is crystal, ya understand. Quite a bit is a blur, and I'd be lyin' if I said I'm not appreciative. Some things man just ain't supposed to remember...that is, if he so desires to maintain at least a shaky grip on sanity. I do recall splatterin' the bodyguard's face but good with that first dose of Demon, a sizeable gob landin' dead center on his right eye. He'd pulled the Glock free and was waivin' it about and staggerin' from side to side while diggin' the fingers of his free hand into his eye. I remember side-steppin' his clumsy lurch while tryin' to draw a bead on King Dimple-cheeks with the other tube.

Guess I underestimated the big man's speed and/or agility, and the next memory I could drudge up was bein' pancaked into the hard wood flooring. I tell ya, if the blow itself hadn't already voided my lungs of oxygen, the less-than-graceful landin' most assuredly did. Can't say where that second tube of skin-peeler flew off to, and at the time I surely wasn't in any condition to search it out. I did, however, have just enough presence about me to notice a shadow loomin' overhead. Seein' that the thing was roughly the size of a Macy's Thanksgiving Day Parade float, there wasn't any ignorin' it. I was definitely a cat's whisker away from bein' stomped into pureed mush by 'Thunder Tee' and his size fourteen shoe. Ya know, it is truly a spiritual awakening to realize you're only seconds away from pushin' up daisies. I reckon I got off three or four quick prayers in that span, though admittedly they were all relatively short and to the point, as in 'save me, lord' or 'see ya in a few, my savior' or some such similar theme.

Well folks, it was about that time that a new character entered the frame. Nah, that ain' t bein' altogether honest. Actually, it was really a familiar character playin' a new part. Ya see, Walt 'Kong' Jenkins, he of the oversized feet of clay, giant shakin' hands, pathetic whimperin' and 'oh god, we're fixin' to die' mentality had been magically jettisoned in the time it'd taken me to take the offensive and be so unceremoniously knocked on my ass. Yep, ol' pussy-fied Walt was gone, replaced by a John Rambo clone that must've beamed in from another galaxy.

Guess it's true what they say about former Jarheads-they never quite lose that gleam to make others scream. Oh, G. I. Kong returned that night, for sure...reenlisted and sure-as-shit twisted...yes sir, returned with a fucking vengeance, pardon my rude 'n crude French. I was finding the simple act of turnin' over on my side a Herculean task, but managed to prop up onto one elbow just as a loud bangin' noise rocked the joint, echoin' through that empty hall like a blast of TNT in a hollow tunnel. I watched Thunder Tee's head swivel violently to one side, blood gushin' forth like H2O from a busted hydrant. The big jackass fell over like an axed oak, no doubt dead as the proverbial hammer long before his bulk hit the stage. Kong tossed the dented B & G aside, reached down and pulled something free from Thunder Tee's motionless carcass, then headed straight for the blinded bodyguard. As calmly as if he were pointin' a finger at a school room blackboard, I saw 'im stick the barrel-end of that Magnum flush against the man's left temple and yank the trigger. Needless to say, Mister Bad-Ass bodyguard no longer had to fret over his lost eyesight.

Rollin' over onto my back, I felt somethin' give and my own vision went a fuzzy gray before a swarm of black dots took command and catchin' my breath was suddenly damn near impossible. Last thing I recall is Kong leanin' over me, the man's expression every bit as granite-jawed and emotionless as it had been ashen-elastic and panic ridden just minutes before.

"You're alright now, Cloudy. Just lay here and catch a breath while I go an' sweep out the rest of the trash..."

I swear to God, that's was the man's exact words-'sweep out the rest of the trash'-weird thing is, I'm sure that's exactly how he meant it.

He wasn't just shovelin' cow pies, neither, as it turned out. By the time I came to surrounded by EMT's, media types, and a busload of flatfoots, the trash had indeed been taken out, big time. According to the first witnesses to arrive on the scene, that being a pair of patrolmen who'd been called out on a 'shots fired' report, Kong had been posed at the complex entrance, all bug-eyed with lips all'a quiver, his head, face and arms coated in blood. The man was reportedly huggin' his dented up B& G to his chest, and when asked what had transpired inside to leave him in such a condition, had smiled that big, dumb crooked grin that was his trademark and commented 'no bug problem here…no sir…not anymore, leastways.''They said he kept repeatin' that same line over and over 'til the medical techs got there and shot 'im up with some industrial strength muscle-relaxer.

Inside they'd found seven bodies all told, two of which had been our former co-workers while another had been the aforementioned complex owner. As for the other four, let's just say Kong had outdone himself in wayward brutality. Upon leavin' me to nap on the stage floor, he'd systematically gunned down both 'Killa Z' Wilkes and the remaining crony and proceeded to drag their bodies onto the stage, stackin' up all four in a neat pile with Thunder Tee reportedly servin' as the foundation.

As for the conclusion of this little nightmare on wheels, think of the scariest horror flick you've ever sat through and wished ya hadn't. Seems Kong, havin' gone way yonder off the deepest end imaginable, had proceeded to soak the bodies in pesticide, collecting all four B&G's and emptying their contents on the pile like he was sprayin' some colossal fire-ant mound. I reckon that solved the mystery tied into his repeated comment about eliminating the 'bug problem' inside the complex.

Needless to say, Kong was hauled away in a separate van than my own; most likely the kind with rubber-padded walls. From what I understand, Wilt permanently resides in a state run booby-hatch somewhere near Waco to this very day, no doubt the recipient of several daily injections. I tried visitin' him once while he was taking up space in the Dallas VA mental ward, but in the three to four minutes we spoke, he held the same glassy-eyed look and never spoke, just kinda gargled and grinned every now and then. Funny, but that trademark smile wasn't the least bit good-natured anymore-more like a snapshot of deep- seeded dementia. I think the poor bastard will be reliving that night for the rest of his born days.

As for me, it ain't like I got off scot-free myself in terms of mental scarring.

I find myself overly paranoid whenever I do a virgin treatment at any out of the way locale, and even then I never enter such premises unarmed. Got my license to carry a few months after the incident, and rarely leave home without blue steel baby at my side. Confidentially, she's packed away in my luggage as we speak. May sound clichéd, but I sure don't take life for granted since that night. Truth is, I'd sworn off firearms after the war. Said I'd never carry again unless my life or those of my loved ones were directly threatened. Talk about your no-brainer reversal in thought process. Anywhow, cliché alert number two; life's a gift from the man upstairs, folks-and nothing, especially years, days and minutes, are guaranteed. That about wraps up story-time…you can swallow those eggs now, Virg.

Everyone seemed to simultaneously pan over and glance at Hobbs, who gulped hard several times before reaching for a tall glass of OJ to wash down whatever had gotten stuck on the way down. The reaction from McCloud's personal rival and harshest critic, that of stilted silence, spoke volumes for the validity of the tale.

Can't speak for the rest, but my own meal tasted a bit stale after that, what few bites I managed to force down in the aftermath. True, we'd all experienced some hairy moments on the job. As a general rule, it came with the territory whenever treating low-income public housing. You either developed a thick outer layer or found another profession. That said, Gaven McCloud had apparently taken a stroll into and out of one of hell's open spaces and lived to tell about it.

The fact that the man was a Medal of Honor recipient who'd seen the horrors of *war* up close made it all the more terrifying that he considered this the worst he'd ever experienced.

There was little doubt in this man's overtly paranoid mind that if things got similarly ugly on this particular mission, I knew exactly who I'd be sticking closest too.

BUG OUT, PART FIVE

Weapons of Mass (Bug) Destruction...

To paraphrase Beth, to whom a client of ours once commented, 'with all these new insects shuffling about, you folks are living on easy street these days,' making a living as a glorified 'bug stomper' wasn't nearly as glamorous in years past. In fact, the 'making a living' part was damn near impossible with the meager wages being doled out. Long work hours and low pay led to a high employee turnover rate, leading to the business as a whole receiving a black eye in terms of reputation.

The industry began to see radical changes in both target enemy and the weapons used to eradicate said foe somewhere after the two-thousand eight presidential election, when long discussed symptoms of Global Warming finally came to the forefront. Symptoms that flat refused to be ignored or pushed to the background any longer. Winters, especially in the Southeast and Southwest, continued to grow shorter and less intense, while summers were just the opposite. I recall thumbing through an issue of Newsweek at my dentist's office during the summer of oh-nine, the lead article of which was entitled *'hell on earth'* and spoke of the serious health hazards tied to living anywhere below the Mason-Dixon line as July temps were reaching near one-hundred twenty on a daily basis. The elderly were already being advised to relocate from such former retirement hubs as Florida, Louisiana and Southern Texas. Believe it was around that time that the first hive of Skin-Bore Ants were officially discovered and subsequently introduced as a 'new and potentially dangerous threat' near Mobile, Alabama. Soon after, it seemed a new species of insect was added almost daily to an already expansive list of hybrid bugs, most of 'em less annoying than potentially lethal. We were no longer simply talking German Cockroaches, bed bugs, termites and millipedes. No sir, the new kids on the block quickly shoved such stalwarts as the Black Widow and Brown Recluse spider to the back of the line in terms of hazardous potential. By two-thousand thirteen, the treatment business was booming, all right, and not just from home and business owners worried about wood, clothing or foundation damage, but from the masses inflicted with a serious case of Entomophobia.

Thing was, by that time it wasn't as much blatant paranoia as cold hard fact. In other words, some real bad mother-hummers had been added to the 'big, bad bug' roll call that folks knew to take seriously from the daily news reports that spoke of the consequences of taking them too lightly. In two-thousand twelve alone, approximately eighteen-hundred people died from the sting of the *Bloat-Belly Scorpion* (most of which originated from the Middle East-The U. S. , for example, chalked up a total of twenty-seven fatalities), while the bite of the *Long- Fanged Pholidae*, or 'Granddaddy Long-Legs', killed a reported forty-six in the Southern United States alone.

There was no talking around the facts-these mutated little bastards had arrived on the scene to kick ass and take names, the majority of 'em hyper-aggressive from the hatching stage, unlike their pre-warming kin. Not to be outdone, the rodent family had its share of newly mutated, disease-spreading kin to add to the roster. Dubbed 'Norway-Mutations', the most common rat in the US had a larger, more aggressive cousin arrive on the scene around two-thousand fourteen. With its muscular flank, pointed, 'Vulcan-like' ears and close-set eyes, the mutant version was easily twice the size of its closest Kin-folk. In this case, unfortunately, additional size also meant a greater capacity to carry and spread at least twice as many diseases. Plus which, the mutated Norway was as hyper-aggressive as the regular model was conflict-shy. Many an amateur rat-hunter had lost a finger, toe, or worst yet, been fatally contaminated by the Norway mutie's oversized, spear-like fangs. Consequently, the cost for rat and mouse baits tripled seemingly overnight. It was about that time that Beth and I had purposely dropped the 'rodent elimination' portion of our ad campaign, though we'd occasionally break regs for a particularly generous client. On the 'control' side of things, pesticide companies were leaping through flaming loops trying to come up with new and improved ways to zap the baddies while being extra cautious in making sure their updated potions wouldn't do the same to those not targeted, that obviously being humans and pets. We'd found out the hard way that what croaked a nest of termites, ants or carpet beetles couldn't make a Giant Assassin Bug or Jagged Centipede sneeze. While such old standbys as Suspend,

Termidor or Speckoz would still eliminate red or black ant colonies, roach nests or Wolf spider colonies when used as directed by State Regs, we were forced to double or sometimes triple legal dosages in order to have the same effect on much smaller infestations of Jamaican Flesh-Eating roaches or Skin-Bore Ants. Though such breeches in state and federal law were conveniently ignored for a bit, it became damned apparent that something had to be done and quick, less any and all exterminators wound up spending the majority of their valuable time in court on poisoning charges than dealing with a fast-spreading epidemic of killer insects. It would be another full year, in May of two-thousand fourteen to be exact, when a whole slew of new chemicals were introduced to the market. By that time, we'd been fighting a losing war for just over two complete flips of the calendar. Talk about having some catching up to do, Beth and I were putting in twelve-hour days, six days a week on a regular basis. Fact was, sixty to seventy hour work weeks were becoming the norm, meaning that keeping a fixed staff of pest control techs was damned near impossible. With the glut of business, especially in the American Midwest and on the East Coast (being that soaring spring and summer temps had caused what came to be known as the 'Great Southern Evacuation' of two-thousand thirteen), new companies were popping up like maggots on a fresh cadaver. Most of 'em went belly up within the first year; predictable since they hadn't considered the cost involved in purchasing new, 'improved' pesticides.

Those that did survive, the larger corporations and such, did so by raising treatment prices in tandem with the rising cost of chemicals. Bottom line was, if the customer wanted the creepy-crawlers to go away, they were gonna have to bite the bullet and pay twenty-first century prices…period. Thus, in raising the overall ante, we as a small company were able to pay our techies a suitable salary and keep a semblance of stability within the ranks. Sure, we ate some profit at first, but once the new chemicals became available and the inevitable price spiral set in as routine, profits within the bug-elimination business soared across the board.

To compare, my first year as a techie waaaaay back at the turn of the millennium garnered me a salary of just under sixteen-hundred bucks a month. These days, the position (entry level) starts out at a cool two and a half grand. Yeah, there's inflation and all that, but still…that ain't exactly peanuts for toting around a lightweight B&G, bait-sprayer and maybe a sack-full of granules. Then again, the modern targets are a helluva lot meaner, not to mention downright treacherous.

***

Around six AM the next morning, we were all treated to freshly-brewed Java and a full-blown breakfast buffet (last meal anyone?) before being shuttled over to the construction site slash state-of-the-art sub-division, where a newly constructed office building would serve as the team's official temporary headquarters.

We were told the squared, red-brick building was to later be utilized as the community administration building, though for the moment it remained mostly bare; just a series of hollowed out, squared offices with windowed walls and very little in the way of furniture.

The conference room was noticeably larger than the one from the previous day's meeting, complete with three separate classroom-type tables, heavily-cushioned stadium seating and a much wider stage area. Peering about, I noticed at least a dozen large mounted speakers hanging about; the kind normally reserved for cinematic consumption.

"Alllll right. This is what I'm talking about," Beth exclaimed while scanning the place with awestruck wonder, "break out the popcorn and soda already."

Taking a corner seat to her right, my whispered response echoed like thunder claps within the almost deafening silence.

"With our luck, it'll be one of those old nuclear war bug-monster flicks."

Maybe it was a subliminal thing, I dunno, but the group seemed set on separation right from the get-go, as no one save Beth and myself chose the same row and sat no closer than three or four chairs from each other. Not exactly joiners, I'd surmise. Like I've said, it's a lonely business. Old habits die hard, no matter the amount of greenbacks being laid on the table.

"Good afternoon, good people of Pest Control," a voice boomed over the speakers, causing every living soul in the room to cringe as one.

The lights dimmed a bit as an individual of obvious small stature strode to the center of the stage.

"Sorry to startle you, folks," the man said, no doubt wearing a mike as a brief squelch of static followed his every spoken word.

"My name is Ronald Godale. I will be your weapons briefer *slash* trainer this fine Ohio morning, as Doctor Bumgartner has fallen ill and is unable to make the trip. We've got quite the overloaded plate, I must say, and only three short hours in which to ensure all of you are thoroughly familiarized with the gadgetry I've brought along. What say we waste no time then on the amenities and get to cooking then? Good…fine and dandelion, as my dear departed Grandfather used to spout…"

The man looked to be in his late forties to early fifties, with thick, gray- streaked hair and a matching goatee that was sharpened to a fine point at its cone-shaped end. Short (no more than five-four or five) and stubby, with a squat, pear-shaped physique, he looked the atypical career cubicle-dweller.

"Now, before the briefing officially starts, let's push all the ego crap to the back-burner, shall we? I'm not here to tell you how to do your respective jobs; your backgrounds speak for themselves. That stated, as you've probably surmised, this isn't your typical pest control assignment. Thusly, the usual weapons of choice do *not*, I repeat, *DO NOT* pertain. It may sound a tad dramatic, but utilizing such methods would truly compare to attempting to take down a bull elephant with an air-rifle. People,

95

we are now treading atop virgin territory. Make no mistake; these grounds are infested. We aren't talking property damage. We're not talking disease or germ migration. We're not even talking bothersome stings or bites that may or may not require medical attention. We're talking the loss of human life in a…most grisly manner. You've seen the pictures…enough said.

Questions abound as to by *what* precisely, and exactly what it will take to quell their apparent reign of terror. Thus, the 'boys at the lab' have outdone themselves to assist you in doing just that. They invent; I train, you learn. Then, if all goes as planned, the seven of you, highly respected professionals all, can go out and wipe up the floor with the grubby little son's of bitches. Now…" he paused, sighing heavily before resuming with a loud hand clap,"…let's all don our thinking caps and pay full attention to the teacher."

"Why, it's gonna seem just like grade school once again, folks. 'Show and Tell', anyone?"

Don't mind confessing that the next hour and a half was nothing short of fascinating. I felt the hair on my arms stand on end numerous times, with my scalp tingling and throbbing with equal fervor. Truly, it was like being a part of one of those old Double-Oh-Seven spy flicks when 'Q' introduced Bond to a grouping of hot-off-the grill secret weapons.

Starting in chronological order, the 'gadget list' included:

96

B & G Turbo Rifles. Lightweight (three pounds). Designed in the same vein as the M-16 rifle. Sprays accurately up to seventy-five feet. Comes with assigned back-pack for holding twin liquid tubes. Each tube holds up to two gallons of pesticide.

NOTE: User MUST wear protective gear. Sprays 'Ultra Suspend, which can peel human flesh upon contact.

Tempo Ultra 'Spears'. Loaded syringes mounted on retractable (up to four feet in length) steel spears. *Intruder Grenades (Cyfluthrin).* Much like a traditional explosive grenade, these detonate exactly ten seconds following pin 'release'. Coats areas up to three-hundred square feet.

NOTE: User MUST wear chemical suit & respirator.

Last but in no way least, we were introduced to what Ron Godale referred to as the Pest Control equivalent to a 'Weapon of Mass Destruction', that being the ….

MaxForce Flusher Unit – Units hold fifteen to twenty-five gallons of a 'pure combination rodenticide/insecticide'. Tech runs reinforced hose/cord to desired location (cord lengths run up to three-hundred feet). Unit is later activated via hand-held remote. Once run sequence is initiated, the unit can thoroughly 'flush' a trouble area as pesticide is sprayed from five separate nozzles, effectively treating up to five-thousand square feet.

NOTE: Minimum safe distance from active 'flushing' is no less than twenty-five yards, though Tech is still required to don protective suit and respirator.

Talk about your 'Sci-Fi' vibes, at that point in the lecture, while standing over the 'Flusher' unit and holding the splayed end of the hose leading to its multiple nozzles, I wouldn't have been shocked to see Captain Marvel himself swoop into the room at full throttle.

"May resemble some sort of alternate universe plumber's helper, son," Godale whispered, seemingly reading my mind while leaning over my left shoulder,"but don't let appearance fool you. I saw up close and personal what that Phantom/Force mix did to a nest of mutant Norway's. Wasn't enough left of those rat-bastards, pardon the pun, to spread on a saltine."

"I take it we consider this a last straw time treatment then?" Beth asked, bending down to inspect the unit, its tiny metallic detonator literally vanishing inside her left palm. Twirling the end of his pointy beard while giving Beth's shapely rear-end a brief once-over, Godale then strolled stiffly away with a subtle arrogance possessed only by those ignorant of their own self-important attitude.

"Oh, not at *all,* miss. But then, we'll be covering plan specifics later this morning."

Tapping those razor-edged titanium nails on each kneecap, Beth glanced up from the unit's outer housing with a barely stifled giggle. I instantly recognized the warped smirk and braced for a heady dose of sarcasm.

"Might as well be toting plastic jugs of Bug-B-Gone on our backs, man.

Like where are the friggin' *blasting caps* already?"

Before I could even attempt to babble an appropriate response, she stood wearing a mask of worry, all good humor having instantly vamoosed.

"Talk to me, Jack-O, you really think any of these cheesy-ass gadgets are gonna save our hides in a pinch?"

Shrugging, I attempted to ease the sudden tension with a tiny portion of humor. Almost always a fatal mistake from an audience appreciation standpoint.

"Well, beats the hell out of hauling around a can of raid and a fistful of termite spikes, right?"

Did I say 'tiny'…more like *microscopic*, at least from my partner's point-of-view.

"That's not an answer, smart-ass," she said, those dark hazel eyes spinning and rolling back like pinwheels. As was the norm whenever I felt myself being treated like a imbecilic crap-for-brains, the nerve she'd touched began throbbing at full tilt.

"Shit, Beth, don't go all worry-wart on me here. Whatever it is, we can handle it. Can't say the extra firepower bothers me, if that's what you mean. I'll take whatever we can get. The stouter the juice, the better."

"The stouter…" she blurted scornfully, executing a textbook 'hair-flip' despite an obvious lack of same,"so you actually trust all these rejects

99

from *Toys R Us* to save our hides when the bug excrement hits the fan?"

At this point, I'm sure my eyes were beginning to bug out even as my Adams Apple shook like a fisherman's bob floating atop swirling lake water.

"Exactly what choice do we have?I get the feeling it's their way or the highway, least you wanna stroll back home broker than when we arrived."

Professor Godale, (nicknamed as such as hours progressed and his tone grew increasingly superior), had just kick-started lecture number two as Beth held up both hands palms up as to quickly make peace between us.

"Whoooa, reel in those nostril flames, dude. Just asking..."

As was the case anytime I stood up for myself or held my ground in any way, the Beth-ster quickly retracted all personal actions and/or previous comments in order to place the 'villain' label squarely between the slumping shoulders of yours truly. It ain't as if this boy needed daily reminders of why we never made it as a couple. There are times that it amazed how the two of us managed to keep a successful business afloat amid the constant emotional chaos and battered baggage from the past. Guess it's one of those rare 'can't live with' but 'can't *work* without' scenarios. In the strange case of Beth and I, it ain't quite 'love/hate', but more along the lines of 'like/oft-times annoyed'. Can't honestly say I don't have feelings for her that run a bit deeper than just skin depth. On the other hand, there's an unspoken understanding between

100

us; a mutual comprehension that anything remotely serious would serve no purpose save screwing up a pretty decent friendship-not to mention one hell of a profitable business partnership. Hotheaded tendencies aside, she was the best damn Tech trainer I ever met, not to mention a pretty savvy businesswoman to boot.

It isn't as if I hadn't thought of flying solo. It's only natural after all. No doubt Beth's done the same. That said, when it comes down to actually making such a bold, possibly reckless move, neither of us possessed the testicular fortitude. Make no mistake, this boy knew where and *from whom* that his bread was buttered.

After a quick demo on each gadget and some one-on-one, hands on training from the 'Prof', we were given the 'smoke 'em if you got 'em' treatment, wherein the lot of us stepped outside the building and into the searing, noontime sun of what we'd been told was an typical late summer Ohio day since the warming process had so drastically altered the local climes. Though pushing ninety-five degrees in mid-September would've been unheard of five years earlier, it was now considered in the mild to warm range, at least when considering the hundred-plus temps that had been the norm just weeks previous.

Feeling the initial symptoms of pore leakage glue the cotton tee firmly between my moistened shoulder blades, I felt a sudden waive of foreboding drive an electrified spike directly between my eyes. Never was much for premonitions and the like.

101

If so, I'd have been wise to take off at a full sprint at that very moment, not daring to turn back until the city limits of New Horizons, Ohio were left miles behind.

102

BUG OUT, PART SIX

Pecking Order Dissention

Congregating in and around a spattering of elm trees (having clearly been recently relocated and replanted) and the wide shade cast by each, I noticed that the short-sleeve shirts donned by both Virgil Hobbs and James Bohannon possessed sizeable sweat circles beneath each arm, while Delbert Prescott's cheeks were plum-colored and gleaming with a thick layer of perspiration.

Oppositely, Gil Braggs and Gaven McCloud both appeared as cool as the proverbial cucumber, each sucking on cancer-sticks while squatting on the nearby curb.

"I must say, is all this…flashy gadgetry really altogether necessary?" Prescott asked aloud, using a bare forearm to wipe the building fop-sweat from his reddish-shaded forehead.

Having blown a series of perfectly symmetrical smoke-rings airborne, McCloud was the first to respond.

"Well, I for one sincerely hope not. Then again, consider the photos of the victims. Thinkin' along those lines, maybe we need all the firepower we can get."

"Techo-garbage, man," Braggs inserted in full wise-ass form, tossing the still smoldering remains of his fag onto the sidewalk and lazily mashing it out with the toe of his boot,"suits just wanna be able to take credit for our kills before cornering the civilian market with safe, 'residential' versions of

103

the same product. It's all about the green, man. Face facts-in the end, we're as expendable as all the dopers, hoes, and crack-fed kids they kicked outta the projects."

Stomping forward like a pissed off storm-trooper, Virgil stood toe to toe with 'Doctor Death', dwarfing the good doc by at least a half a foot.

"If that's your opinion, man, just what the hell are you doing here?"

"You can't be that dense, Hobbs," Braggs replied, holding both hands palms out and slowly curling the fingers back,"same reason you are. It sure as shit isn't to help save humanity or clear this burg for the suits new modern marvels of architecture. It ain't even for the free pub we're apt to garner in the aftermath. No, let me chalk it up for you with four simple words: *Cold...hard...green...backs*."

Nodding in apparent disgust, Hobbs side-stepped away with his hands parked atop his hips.

"Speak for yourself, mister. Personally, I'm all about new challenges and the conquest thereof. Money is, and always has been, secondary to the task at hand."

Feigning masturbation by wildly pumping his left fist, Braggs wisely ceased the gesture once Hobbs had turned back his way for a final word.

"If that's your attitude, do me a favor and just keep your distance. You got carelessness written all over you."

"Ah, come now gents," Prescott intervened, stepping to center stage in a parade-rest pose.

"We have no bloody choice but work together to achieve mission success, agreed?"

"You tell 'em, Coach," McCloud cracked, lighting up yet another smoke.

Leaning against the same steel door we'd all exited, Bohannon crossed his arms ('mutated pythons' Beth had later referred to 'em) across his barrel- shaped chest and sighed in apparent disgust. Mister 'Happy-Go-Lucky' he wasn't.

"Damned if it isn't like being stuck with a group of bickering fifth graders fighting over whose daddy is the biggest bad-ass. This has all the potential of being the longest two days in recorded history."

I saw Beth's mouth part as to put in her two cent's worth, normally a sarcasm-laced, potentially combative verbal contribution I usually anticipated with root-canal dread, when the 'Prof' mercifully saved the day by tapping on a nearby classroom window as to prod us back inside. The next three and a half hours were spent not only plotting the impending mission, but also creating an unofficial pecking order within the ranks.

In addition to his weapons briefing, it seemed Professor Godale had been chosen to lay down the law, so to speak, on what specific Chain of Command the suits had decided upon.

Not surprisingly, and more than likely due to our 'tag-team' status, Beth and I found ourselves secured firmly atop the bottom rung, essentially bringing up the rear. Safe to say neither of us had a problem with being slighted, as being woefully underestimated had become part of our MO through the years. Truth be told, we'd effectively used such treatment as a motivational tool since opening the business and shoving some of the 'big boys' around in the process.

All that said, New Horizon's choice for our unofficially leader 'in the trenches' did set off a sensitive nerve or two within the ranks. To the others credit however, most of 'em managed to show their obvious disapproval via non- verbal clues such as slight frowns or wide-eyed scowls. All, that is, save one.

You got it; that master of civil maturity, the good doctor himself.

"Ah, fuck that noise, bud. What rates *him* above all the rest…specifically me?"

"The decision is final, Mister Bragg," the Prof replied, already having averted his eyes from the ranting little jack-ass and back to the virtual black-board and the bulleted mission outline,"now, lets discuss the plan of action step by step until it is literally engraved within the very brain stem itself."

"Hey man, don't ignore me like I'm some ignorant street tech," Bragg continued, his whiny tone growing increasingly shrill and feminine by the syllable.

"Hobbs doesn't have anything on me expect maybe his advanced years. I'm worth a cool million, pal, with two more branches on the way as we speak. If anybody qualifies to lead this group of overrated pinheads into the pits, it's yours truly…the doctor of death."

After a moment's pause, wherein an equal mix of giggles and groans permeated the room, it was

Gaven McCloud who responded while Hobbs, the target of Bragg's bone-headed rant, remained surprisingly indifferent.

"Doc, in speakin' for the rest of the overrated pin-heads present, allow me to prescribe somethin' for this terminal case of bitchin' ya seem to be afflicted by..."

McCloud turned slowly in Bragg's direction with his fists clinched tightly at his sides. The man's squinting eyes were ablaze with rage; his jaw muscles clinching and flexing with equal fervor. It was a side of Gaven McCloud I'd yet to witness, and at that moment I'd have wagered even big, bad James Bohannon felt a twinge of intimidation, however slight.

"Keep it up, boy, and I'll order up a Max-Force enema made just for you."

"I...you can't th-threaten..." Braggs spat, his pasty complexion having already transformed into about three separate shades of maroon.

"Listen up, shit-for-brains..." McCloud broke in sternly, though managing to keep his overall tone remarkably calm, like a wise elder scolding an insubordinate child,"if I ain't got a problem with Virgil blazing the trail, *no one* should."

"I...you can't talk to me that wa-. . ."

McCloud took a single, purposeful step into the aisle, causing Bragg to flinch as if he'd been slapped firmly across the forehead with an open palm.

"Hit the mute button, kid...and keep it engaged 'til further notice, ya read? No one wants to hear any more of your whiny bullshit."

107

Wisely, the good doctor complied, proving he possessed just enough common-sense to perhaps salvage his own ass. Slumping into his chair with a low grunt, Braggs truly resembled a scolded five-year old with his pouting lips and squinting gaze. It was all I could do not to openly guffaw.

As Professor Godale had explained it, the New Horizons hierarchy had deemed it necessary to appoint what he referred to as a 'lead person' to head up the project once the team arrived at ground zero. After what he termed several 'tension-filled' discussions, the mantel of leadership would be given to Virgil Hobbs for the duration of the mission.

As for the aforementioned chain of command, Delbert Prescott was chosen second in command, followed by Gaven McCloud and James Bohannon. Being that the list petered out before our names were ever even mentioned, that relegated Beth and I to 'platoon leader' and 'platoon', not necessarily in that order. No biggie, we later agreed. *Grunts* at heart, we were, regardless of how healthy our bank accounts had become through the years. Ask any tech who'd ever been in our employ; Beth and I had always been the 'hands-on' types that never asked more from our subordinates than we were willing to do ourselves.

Assholes? Perhaps…periodically. As a boss, it's *mandatory* at times. But lazy, contented or complacent? Never has happened and ain't apt too in this lifetime. If anyone said so, they were a lying SOB with a personal axe to grind, period.

"Guess you two will be bringin' up the rear, Ace," McCloud whispered, reaching up to lightly tap my right shoulder.

Leaning back as far as the high-back chair would allow, I managed a weak shrug.

"Not a problem, my man. Story of my life."

"I feel you, dude. Truthfully, I'd rather be back there with ya. Just the pressure of playin' third-fiddle is already tightenin' my gut."

As alluded to earlier, I knew right from the get-go that Gaven McCloud was what my grandpa used to refer to as a 'good egg'. Being that remainder of the 'crew' seemed to consist of either tight-ass egomaniacs (Bohannon, Hobbs) or equally self-important Jackasses (Bragg), it was a comfort to share space with the likes of him and the ever-positive, always chipper Mister Prescott.

As for the plan itself, simplicity seemed to the byword, at least on the surface. Nothing more elaborate than a series of routine foundation treatments really, just on a larger scale with more bodies and equipment involved.

According to the three-dimensional blue-prints on display, there were seven separate buildings to cover, housing a grand total of fourteen town-homes. Of those, three were scaled almost to completion with in-tact crawl spaces, while the remaining were skeleton models at best, at least up top. At first glance, it seemed no more than a two to three hour job. That is, until we all got a better look at the highlighted particulars associated with those prints. Beth must've been the first to notice, as her initial groan superseded what was soon to become a chorus.

"Holy shit, who designed these things, Willy Freaking Wonka?" Doc Braggs grumbled, though his tone was conspicuously acid-free, bordering on positively mild.

"Are those…what I think they are?" Hobbs asked, comically wide-eyed while rotating a pointing finger to three specific points of the brightly-lit screen.

"Looks like access points of some kind, complete with entry doors and key pads," Bohannon added in that ultra-husky voice that made the late, great Barry White sound positively feminine.

"What they got stowed away down there, chief, a diamond mine?" McCloud inquired, though without a trace of actual humor.

Leaving his chair, it took Hobbs but two lengthy strides to place himself directly in front of the screen. The man practically had his face pressed to the display before backing quickly away and posing with his chin propped atop a clinched fist.

"Where are those passages leading to? Nucleus looks like a goddamned bunker."

"Quite spacious, I must say," Prescott added calmly, the lone voice of reason who was too quickly dismissed.

"Bunker my ass," Braggs chimed in, this time with his normal dose of smarmy cockiness,"you could park a double-decker RV in that hole."

McCloud's head flew back as raucous laugher split the air, though the overall effect did little to soften the building tension.

"Nail on the head, Virg, as always, nail directly on the head! Potential clients, filthy rich SOB's one and all, must want a place to hide away and play mole in case of some Middle Eastern Nuke action."

The Prof scoffed, waiving both hands about in a pausing gesture."Nothing as secretive, I'm afraid, though in terms of overall value you're not that far off, Mister McCloud. In fact, I'd venture to say what is being protected twenty feet below surface level might easily be the most vital cog within the compound's inner workings."

After a short pause, wherein I'm sure the Prof was mentally prepping a freshly stacked slew of clichés with which to bedazzle and bombard us, Beth broke her relatively lengthy silence (at ten-plus minutes, it was fast-approaching record levels).

"*Compound,* huh? Jeez Teach, I'm beginning to detect the distinct aroma of government involvement in this here project. Are you sure we being straight- talked here? I mean, is there something else we should kn-..."

"My lady...*please,*" the Prof broke in with just the briefest of sneers that quickly reverted back to a tight, wholly insincere smile. Apparently, she'd struck just the right nerve and the old man had accidentally fell out of character for the first time.

"There is no secretive agenda at work here, of that I can *assure* you. It's as simple as this; nineteen buildings containing a total of thirty-eight housing units are slated to be complete within the next two months. The ribbon on this upscale community, or *compound* if one prefers, is set to be cut with no less than the governor of this great state present.

111

Contracts state that when and only when construction is complete on *all* thirty-eight town-homes and all state inspections have been successfully passed will the new inhabitants be allowed to occupy said units."

Despite the calm mannerisms and silky-sooth tone, I had a feeling the man was still clearly irked at Beth's less-than-subtle acquisition. Company man all the way, Professor Godale didn't at all appreciate the team's overall attitude, least of which I'm sure was the underlying layer of distrust.

"Now, if any of you feel dissatisfied with my answers and wish to null and void their individual contracts, please do so before our little field trip to the compo-um, that is, the site. In that event, the corporation will choose one of the alternate tech's as a team substitution."

With that, everyone in the room turned toward Beth in an almost comically synchronized double-take.

"Hey, don't look at me," she said, flashing 'peace signs' with both raised hands,"I'm aboard this here bug-train for good."

Once the group's focus had been re-trained back to the Prof, she flashed me a 'what did I do?' shrug, to which I matched a shoulder twitch of my own, though unable to completely wipe away the grin that accompanied it. There were instances when being that woman's partner was a real hoot, though guilt by association was at times a heady price to pay.

"Very well then," the Prof chirped a bit too enthusiastically for my taste."Now that we're all back on the same page, let me fully explain the reasons for those underground entry points."

The remainder of the briefing took a full two hours, the majority of that covering the treatment plan scheduled for the next morning. As for the so-called 'bunker', it didn't turn out to be anything quite as elaborate. The Architects who'd designed the community had decided to construct the neighborhood's power grid underground as to avoid any present and future vandalism from ex-tenants or potential intruders looking for an easy mark-i. e, shut down the grid for robbing and looting purposes. Such 'hideaway hubs', as the Prof referred to 'em, had become pretty much status quo in upscale sub-divisions within the past several years, though none of us had ever seen a grid set-up of such magnitude.

Damned thing took up at least three-thousand square feet, with three separate, winding tunnels leading from the surface to its core thirty-five feet below.

The grid wasn't just about a power source, either, but also contained a state of the art computer hub and, just as Virgil had hinted, four separate ten by twelve shelters in case of natural or 'man-made' disasters. Sign of the times it seemed. The 'cold-war' of the twentieth century had seen the birthing of similar fall-out shelters, a fad that history books stated faded into apparent oblivion, at least until the Middle Eastern debacles of late, wherein at least a half-dozen countries and/or assorted terrorist groups had made the good ol' US of A a steady target of threats the government no longer deemed as casual.

So, for those paranoid mini-masses with the extra funds to spare, constructing reinforced concrete and steel bunkers in back yards had once again become all the rage.

Apparently, the good folks at New Horizons had seen fit to add what the Prof called 'Failsafe Rooms' as an added amenity-an amenity that would certainly hike the asking price by a few thousand or so per unit. Only thing was, access to the bunkers was limited to three locations within the community; the sub-division's rec room and gymnasium located at the site's eastern edge; the community meeting hall from the west, and from the relatively small, single-story building we were presently occupying, located smack-dab in the middle of the site that the Prof referred to as 'Admin HQ'. This was apparently where the manager and maintenance staff's offices would be located, along with the community post office.

At this point, I recall a few of us, the Prof included, pausing just long enough to peer down at the floor beneath our feet, as if already sizing up the as- of-yet unseen opposition.

"Now he tells us," Beth quipped, scowling sourly and shuffling her boots about as if standing in an active fire-ant hill.

"I knew my ass-cheeks were itching for a reason," I replied, and saw her scowl transform into a warped grin. As always, it was never less than a joyful hoot whenever I found a way to tickle her fancy, short-lived as the moment was.

"I don't quite comprehend the logic of such a layout," Delbert Prescott had said at one point,

114

gesturing towards the display with a cocked eyebrow.

"Wouldn't it have been a more…attractive offer to have passages leading from each building to the fallout shel-um, rooms? I mean, from a tenants standpoint the matter of a convenient access seems to be a rather serious issue."

As if prepped for such an inquiry, the Prof didn't miss a beat, spewing forth an explanation that sounded as rehearsed as the most polished political speech.

"In truth, Mister Prescott, the initial blueprints did call for exactly such a set-up. As it turned out, however, the housing committee at New Horizons feared that some future tenants might see this as a bit…well…overtly paranoid. Not only that, but they were also informed by a team of industrial engineers that such an elaborate series of tunnels might well weaken the sub-structures of not only the town-homes, but also the landscape itself. Thus, it was decided to station the three tunnels at strategic areas in and around the homes, thereby providing sufficient access from all directions."

Dialogue pretty much petered out after that, and we were treated to lunch at a nearby Mexican Buffet before returning for what the Prof called a pre-game 'walk-through' of the Hot Zone. As the final stage of mission prep commenced, I have to admit feeling a stout case of what a former co-worker of mine used to call the 'Heebie-Jeebies'. I'm talking creep-out city-and bone-marrow deep at that. If I were to speculate (not one of my more dependable traits, I have to say), I'd have chalked it up to a combination of things, not the least of which were those pureed corpse pics we'd been shown. Strange place-strange people-even *stranger* potential enemy or enemies. Combine all that and the fact that few of us so-called 'professional exterminators' (save McCloud and perhaps Prescott) really had a blessed clue how'd we react in the face of actual life-threatening danger, and it was a damn wonder my hands weren't visibly shaking as our mission walk-through began.

BUG OUT, PART SEVEN

Into the Hot Zone...the Prequel

"Just to ease your mind a bit, folks," Professor Godale began as we circled the admin building in single-file, no doubt resembling a line of weary storm- troopers policing a virgin location. A light rain had began to fall, and I welcomed each semi-cooled drop as it smacked my face and bare arms, knowing full well that the result of such random precip would likely be humidity thick enough to carve with the dullest of butter knives. Regardless, it was the first wet-stuff I'd seen fall from the arid sky in weeks, and I felt instantly re-charged in its wake.

"New Horizons has hired the Honor Guard security firm to insure you will not be entering the three marked locations without armed escorts. Reason being of course is the spattering of former inhabitants who seem to permeate the area after dark for no other reason than to initiate various mayhem in and around their former neighborhood. You folks need only worry about the bugs, while the Honor Guard associates will deal with any potential human issues."

"Can you believe some people?' I heard James Bohannon grumble to my left,"kicked out into the street like so much bagged trash and they still have the *audacity* to hold a grudge?" It was easily the longest stretch of dialogue we'd heard from the 'Eradicator' since the team had been assembled, his sarcasm- laced blurb delivered with all the emotion

117

of a freshly plucked turnip. Then again, perhaps that was as revved up as the man got. If so, I couldn't help but give silent thanks that the man seemed the polar opposite of good ol' Doc Death, who managed to say less with more words than any person I'd ever come across.

We entered a well-lit, railed stairwell from the rear of the building and descended in single-file.

"The first of three lock-down points is about forty-steps down," the Prof informed, blazing the old trail at a deliberate pace as to allow us a feel of the place. As far as an initial vibe, I couldn't work up much in the way of dread. After all, you see one stone-encased stairwell, you've pretty much seen 'em all.

"Entry will be accessed past each point via your security escorts, who will be granted the applicable access codes."

As we trudged on, the natural bug-snuffer in me took over as I couldn't help but scan every nook and cranny for evidence of potential prey. About thirty or so steps down, guard post number one (so dubbed by Beth later that evening) swam into view beneath the bright fluorescent lighting. At that point, I hadn't spotted so much as a hollowed husk, detached limb or stain-dried slug trail to hint at a possible infestation. Maybe they'd recently cleaned the well, though logically that made about as much sense as scooping a single elephant turd from a full herds droppings.

The well widened dramatically as we faced the sealed entry/exit door, and the group quickly spread into a semi-circle as the Prof again took center stage.

"Up until a few days ago, we would've normally been greeted at this point by an armed guard inquiring today's password."

Nudging back a few steps as to give everyone visual access to the wall space just to the left of the door, he pointed out a mounted, numerical keypad.

"Once the correct password had been established, a five digit entry code would then be utilized. Know this people, less than a dozen people had been granted these codes, most notably the chief electrician and computer administrator. Once the...disappearances began, not one but two separate security firms were hired and resigned from said posts. We...that is, the company, were fortunate that Honor Guard has accepted the task at hand, considering the...mysterious disappearances which plagued the previous security firm."

His first few words echoing off the walls of the confined space like cannon- fire, Gaven McCloud winced before lowering the volume several decibels.

"Yeah, and I'll bet they paid out their collective asses to get 'em down here, at that."

The Prof tilted his head to one side, biting his lip as to suppress a less jovial response.

"As with you fine professionals, they are being very well compensated...yes."

"Uh-huh," McCloud replied with a wink, "guess I should say touché, Teach."

"Cut the BS, Cloudy," Hobbs growled, moving forward and placing his right hand flat against the steel door as if checking it for heat or vibrations from the opposite side. A decidedly strange bird, this Virgil Hobbs character-cocky as the day was long, but also as intense and dedicated to task as any I'd seen. Still, only time would tell whether the mystery board's choice of him as group leader would turn out to be either a wise one or perhaps a flat-out lemon, the latter of which possibly being hazardous to our collective health.

"What the hell you doin', Virg, a Vulcan mind-meld?" McCloud snickered, leaning hard to his left to playfully nudge Bohannon on the shoulder. The other man's sneering, comically stoic reaction was priceless, like somebody had just thumped his testicles.

I saw Beth's lips part and her left hand begin to rise as to pose a question just as Delbert Prescott beat her to the verbal punch.

"So, my good man, once this door is accessed, what is the distance to the next level?"

"Twenty-five additional steps. Once penetrated, the third and last stop- gap blockade is only fifteen before the power grid's nucleus is successfully breached."

"So we're supposed to treat on the way down to the grid or on the way back up?" 'Doc' Braggs injected in what was essentially a strained whisper. The dude's ball-sac had definitely been deflated since that last briefing. As for his question, I saw both Beth and McCloud roll their eyes in almost perfect unison.

"Logically Mister Braggs, you would need to reach the grid and work your way back up as to avoid overexposure to the chemicals yourselves. Remember, folks, these poisons are ten-fold stout in terms of the watered-down versions you're used to. Even with chemical suits and respirators, the less exposure the better."

"Jeez, *Einstein* you ain't, pal," McCloud barked with obvious disdain,"how long since you got those manicured hands dirty in the field, son?"

"Fuck off, man," Braggs retaliated, though he'd wisely backed up the stairwell a few steps before doing so,"just want all my ducks in a row, that's all."

Reaching up to scratch his lightly bearded chin, McCloud's peered over at Virgl Hobbs, his expression the textbook definition of wry.

"*That* one's all yours, Virg. Break out the virgin techie manual, Dude. It's definitely back to training day numero-uno for some people."

Leaning back against the sealed door, the Prof was sporting the haggard look of the terminally fed up.

"Children, please. I'm beginning to believe it's a good thing you'll be split into three teams for the mission's initial phase."

"So all three tunnels, um, passageways are identical?" Beth asked, hugging her bare arms across her chest as if suddenly chilled.

"Identical, yes. Thus, one three person team and a pair of two-person units per passage, not counting the security personnel who will accompany each, at least until you reach the power grid room."

121

Always the 'take-charge' guy, at least according to Gaven McCloud, team leader in theory Hobbs inquired next, no doubt figuring it was no less his 'duty'.

"As for those...MaxForce Flusher Units, which tunnel and/or team gets the honor?"

"Good question, Master Hobbs," the Prof replied with what might've been mock cheer as he pushed away from the door and sauntered past the group in order to jog back up the first set of stairs. In true 'Barney Fife' fashion, Virgil Hobbs' smug, 'I know I'm the man' expression in wake of the Prof's comment was equally comical and stomach-churning. Just as first impressions had hinted at Gaven McCloud's favorable character, Virgil Hobbs 'Natural-Born Jackass' persona actually seemed to worsen over time.

"Team three...that is the group containing three members would be the most logical, as would this particular tunnel as the grounds above are not nearly as cluttered with construction materials."

"Speaking of the individual pairings, we...that is, the corporation, feels it only fair this be a group decision. Break it down anyway you'd like," he paused, smiling grimly while eyeing McCloud and 'Doc' Braggs in particular.

"Remember folks, this isn't about heroics or media glory in the aftermath.

It goes without saying that unless the mission is a complete success that any favorable PR towards your individual businesses is, of course, an impossibility."

Everyone seemed to pick that specific moment to shuffle their feet and avoid eye contact, like grade-school kids in a class play shying away from an opening night curtain.

Guess the Prof's words, cold-hard fact they stated, hit home to us all. Just as life in general was rarely considered fair and just, the grim truth was spelled out in bold crayon for all to behold. Limp away from this particular job a failure and every rival in the business would use it as a recruiting tool both to steal customers and drag our company names through the boggiest mudslide imaginable. Alternately, kicking some major bug-ass might well have the opposite effect on the financial bottom line, as well as some glowing word-of- mouth from an ad standpoint.

In fact, New Horizons contracts had stated that in lieu of a successful site cleaning, the possibility of internet and local cable TV ads was a definite maybe for each company involved.

"Alright, people, this is as far as we go this day. We'll wrap things up with a final refresher before tying on the old feedbag and dismissing you for the evening. Back to the surface then," the Prof announced before whirling about and pouncing up the stairs two at a time as if darting away from rising flames.

Not sure about anyone else, but the energetic bounce of a half-hour earlier had left this boy's step as we headed north. *Rubber-legged* and *cement brained*, as Beth loved to spout whenever I feel into one of my self-imposed dazes.

For some reason, my focus was trained solely on which mini-team I'd be assigned to, and hoping like hell that the same roster wouldn't contain the names 'Doc' Braggs or Virgil Hobbs. Juvenile as it sounded, I'd have willingly traded Beth as a potential teammate just to avoid sharing tunnel space with those two sore-headed assholes. You know what they say, whoever in blue blazes *they* is; sometimes you get what you wish for, and live to regret it.

BUG OUT, PART EIGHT

Suiting up for War

"Best damn steak and taters I've had in eons," McCloud exclaimed in the wake of a booming belch that caused ripples to form in the beer mug sitting to my right. I lie to you not, it was at least a level five on the old burp-meter Richter scale. Very impressive indeed, though I could tell by Beth's appalled expression that she was less than thrilled.

"Didn't know they had the skills to sizzle up such a tasty slap of beef up here in Yankee country. No doubt imported from the Lone Star state."

I'd finished off my second turkey sub just moments earlier, washing it down with a frosty Coors light. Having separated themselves (purposely perhaps) from the team, 'Professor' Ron Godale and 'Pretty Boy' Floyd Garrison sat a full four booths ahead, each nursing unidentifiable cocktails while rarely exchanging either dialogue or even the occasional glance. The casual observer might've thought them complete strangers by their void, disinterested expressions. To me it was more a matter of two company men forced to share a meal at the boss's expense. Each had that 'let's get this cornball shit over with and get our butts home already' look about 'em. Not exactly inspiring from a 'new employee' point of view. Then again, our ragtag 'group' was nothing more than overpaid temps to such as they; quick-fix guns for hire who were as faceless and immaterial as they were expendable.

The place was called 'The Dine-In Revue', a relatively small, off-the- beaten path eatery slash pub that we'd been assured had quite the rep among the locals. Being that it was just after eight PM on a Friday night and our little group was the establishment's lone customers, it was fairly obvious that New Horizons had rented the joint exclusively for their newest hires.

"Above-average grub all right. Sure beats the hell outta Micky D's," I responded just as a rather buxom waitress of the Hispanic nationality floated by to put a head on my brew.

Delbert Prescott, sharing a booth with the ever tight-lipped James Bohannon just to our left, echoed similar sentiments in his own unique verbiage.

"I must concur, good sir. Though I must admit to being a bit weary at first, what you yanks refer to as…catfish was no less than ab-so-tively smashing. I dare wonder if an act of bribery might procure me the recipe for future gorging."

"Ah yes, the condemned eat a hearty meal," Beth blurted, spitting out a flurry of fragmented nacho chips in the process. Milking her third Long Island Ice Tea in the past hour, her eyelids were developing that hang-dog look I unfortunately knew so well. No ifs, ands or buts, there was the distinct possibility I'd be hoisting her over my shoulder in the textbook 'soldiers carry' before the night was over. Certainly wouldn't be the first time, but that didn't make the prospects any less unattractive.

Leaning back from the table directly across from the booth McCloud, Beth and I shared, Doc

Braggs blew thick, lingering smoke trails from each nostril.

Though his face remained out of view, I could still envision the sneer accompanying the words.

"The voice of optimism rears its drunken head. So typical of your overachieving female types."

Suddenly wide-eyed, Beth calmly gulped down the remains of the tea before shrieking angrily and slamming the tall glass against the table top. Damn thing exploded into a thousand shards, and I'm pretty damned sure I was the lone soul stationed within twenty feet of that booth that didn't openly cringe.

Nothing to brag about really…I'd simply seen it countless times before. The term 'shell-shocked' has many variations, some of which have little or nothing to do with battlefield experiences.

"You mind repeating that, Gil?" she huffed with nostrils flaring, shoving the table forward 'til it rammed a comically shocked Gaven McCloud at breast- bone level, then practically body-slamming me to one side as to depart the booth and strike a fighting pose. She hadn't yet bothered to step forward, instead waiting on Doc 'Moron' to make the next move, if any.

"This pessimistic, overachieving female type needs to see up close and personal if such a strong, stalwart male possesses the *ball-sac* immense enough to spout such a steaming pile of twentieth-century, chauvinistic horseshit to her face."

Wisely, Braggs didn't budge. Fact is, he didn't even bother to turn around, likely figuring that doing so might result in a few broken bones and/or teeth. Again, surprising intelligence from one so blatantly stupid the majority of the time.

"Whoaaaa there, Cambridge. Just tweaking your strings is all. *Damn*, doesn't anyone here own the deed to a working sense of humor?"

"Ain't it amazing how a foot that size can fit so snugly inside that boy's jaws?" McCloud said, wincing a bit while massaging his battered chest.

"Figured as much," Beth groaned, her fists still balled tightly in pre-strike mode. I'd seen the woman take on men who outweighed her by a hundred pounds and a foot-plus in height. Come to think of it, those were usually the occasions I ended up with either badly bruised ribs, a split lip, or a slight concussion from playing rescuer for her drunken ass.

"Chicken-shit, weasel-wicked big mouth. In other words, just your *typical* male."

This time there was no stopping, at least completely, the torrent of laughter that spewed forth. Actually, I'm not altogether sure I even tried that hard to refrain. Cocky little jackass deserved the ridicule. Besides, it wasn't as if I were the only one. Hell, even Delbert Prescott, the man once knighted by a queen no less, briefly flashed a wide, cheesy grin in the aftermath of Bragg's well-deserved comeuppance.

The remainder of mealtime sailed by without incident and with a minimum of dialogue. Maybe it was pre-mission jitters or just a matter of individual mental preparation, but by the time we'd arrived back at the hotel at just before eight PM, even the normally chatty Gaven McCloud had grown solemn and morose. Less than ten hours from kick-off, so to speak, and already 'game faces' were being tried on for good measure.

Though not by any means my usual behavior the eve before such a task, I emptied several mini-bottles of firewater before sacking out, including a double- shot of one-fifty-one rum that seared my breastbone and set my gut ablaze.

Sleep, when it did come, was fitful at best. Though being overly apprehensive wasn't a virgin trait to this boy when high levels of pressure were involved, this had been on a radically larger scale altogether. I've talking nightmares of the beyond bizarre variety, most of which were inundated with visions of ripped, shredded or pulped flesh and bloody, steaming viscera. Talk about your prophetic premonitions. Always heard hindsight was twenty-twenty. Oh well, no such animal as 'inner-minds eye' corrective surgery, I guess.

***

Digital alarm sounded off at straight up five AM, as set by the same mildly hung-over Pest Control Specialist/Business co-owner that was just hours away from following a slightly winding staircase straight down into the fiery pits of Hades hell itself. Melodramatic I know, but if the description fits…live it.

We had awoken the next morning to muggy, humid conditions, stout winds from the West and an overcast sky. The only thing missing from the 'fictional foreboding' checklist was a lingering fog swirling about near our ankles.

At just minutes before six, following a continental breakfast consisting of glazed donuts, fresh fruit, and steaming hot java, the team converged inside the now familiar conference room to suit up for battle. On our way in, I spotted a trio of newer model, black Ford sedans with dark-tinted windows parked at the Eastern edge of the building. On the side of each read 'Honor Guard – *Your Welfare and Security is OUR Business*' in a deep shade of maroon. Seemed our armed escorts had arrived, though for some strange reason I felt no less insecure.

Both Professor Godale and Pretty Boy Garrison were present for the suiting up, the former providing us with a final run-through on correct procedures for weapons use. Perhaps under looser, less stressful circumstances, we all might've split a lip howling at our own appearance in the aftermath of donning said gear. My own personal evaluation placed us somewhere between the '*Ghostbusters'* and the storm-troopers from the original *Star Wars* flicks.

On the positive side, the body suits and accompanying hand-weaponry were relatively lightweight.

On the downside, the combination of respirator, facemask and hard- helmet made my noggin feel about as buoyant as a wrecking ball. I saw Beth openly struggle with both the respirator and plastic-dome mask, fidgeting madly in order to find just the right fit. Gaven McCloud, on the other hand, appeared downright thrilled-like a kid dressing up to play cowboy. The rest were hard to read, though I noticed *Commander* Hobbs studying each of us at separate times, as if to ensure his assigned 'troop' were donning their gear strictly by the book.

As for the aforementioned gear, each of us donned a spandex-type body suit that the Prof assured was leak-proof as well as 'chemically retardant' from a pesticide standpoint. He did add that the protective suit was only effective for 'light to medium' exposure. In other words, do a swan dive into a vat of Suspend Ultra and the suit material would most likely melt away along with the majority of one's flesh, muscle and sinew.

"Oh, Super-duper...behold stew techie gumbo," McCloud cracked upon hearing that particular tidbit, igniting a nervous giggle or two from the mostly subdued crowd.

If nothing else, the suits did provide some much-needed comic relief.

Dark blue with bright yellow striping that ran from the armpit down the sides of each leg, it was as if they'd been commandeered from a local scuba-diving surplus store. At least the damn things didn't come with a skin-tight skull-cap intact, though that was sadly the *lone* saving grace.

Comments (mostly whispered save in the case of James Bohannon, whose gravelly tone simply won't comply) ranged from Delbert Prescott's 'utterly ridiculous' to Gaven McCloud's 'damn thing sure highlights my beer gut' to Bohannon growling 'who the hell sized these things? Feels like my balls are locked in a vice. ' In my eyes, Bohannon had little to bitch about. With his meticulously toned, body-builder physique and overstuffed groin region, he was one of the few

131

whom the two-sizes-two-small suit actually flattered. No lie-the man looked like a comic-book superhero come to life. Captain *Constipation,* perhaps?

Beth, with her ample bosom, taunt but not overly muscular thighs and shapely rear rated as a close runner-up in the 'swimsuit competition'.

Meanwhile, a terminal case of chicken-legs, accompanied by a slightly bloated gut and concave chest (unfortunately a family trait) labeled yours truly as the non-athletic type by proxy. Sad, but at least I wasn't in a class by myself. Not in any particular order, the rather pathetic specimens on display included:

Gil 'Doc' Braggs – The man's twig-arms, round shoulders and rail-thin calves teamed with size thirteen boots brought to mind a second-string comic book hero gone tragically to seed.

Gaven McCloud – Despite an impressive set of canons and broad, chiseled shoulders that spoke of a life-long weight lifter, the sizeable midsection he patted with (mock?) pride overshadowed all positive aspects.

Virgil Hobbs – Though he didn't appear altogether out-of-shape, our fearless leader possessed a gangly, off-kilter build that was the definition of in- proportionate.

Delbert Prescott – No doubt considered quite slim and trim for his advanced years, our resident Brit nonetheless suffered the sure-fire symptoms (sagging gut, lack of youthful muscle tone) of a mid-life curse some refer to as 'male-melting'. Still, despite my cohorts many and varied physical shortcomings, I wasn't exactly searching out a vanity mirror myself.

As McCloud so eloquently put it just as equipment hand-out continued, 'the *Mighty Avengers* we ain't.'

Respirators and face-masks were next on the agenda-the former the double filtered type-the latter complete with clear plastic, smear-proof lenses and triple straps (scalp; back of skull; neck). Nothing out of the ordinary here, as we'd all worn similar devices during routine fog or dusting jobs. One addition to the face-marks was a tiny, built-in com device that would allow all three teams to communicate once separated into the separate passageways. This particular gem had '*I'm Virgil Hobbs, team leader, and you're not*' written alllll over it. Just a hunch, you understand.

Next to be issued were the B & G turbo rifles complete with pesticide-filled backpack, the latter of which attached via leather-banded shoulder and chest harnesses. Falling onto one knee in the classic shooters pose, Beth pointed the front site my way and fired off several practice shots. Apparently satisfied with the weapon's potential workability, she winked my way before slinging it over one shoulder. Regulation B & G metallic canister sprayers were next, each of which held a gallon and a half of a Demon-X/BP-400 mix usually reserved for spraying large hives of Assassin bugs or Skin-Bore ants.

The Tempo Ultra Spears came next, and we all took turns practicing the downward 'whip' motion that retracted the slim baton body and syringed tip.

It was like a scene from every prison flick you'd ever seen where a group of 'screws' readied themselves for an impending inmate riot.

Intruder Grenades were slapped into our palms soon after. Roughly the size of a regulation baseball and nearly as lightweight, the Prof nonetheless reminded us ad nausea of the dangers involved in case of premature detonation.

As for the last resort-the 'weapon of mass bug destruction' as McCloud had dubbed it, the MaxForce Flusher Unit was handed over to Virgil Hobbs for official designation, along with the accompanying hose (three-hundred feet worth) rolled tightly onto a hard-plastic casing and the 'detonator', which resembled nothing more elaborate than a palm-sized remote control. It may sound chicken-shit, but I didn't want anything to do with that bad-boy, and it wasn't just a matter of responsibility. Honestly, I was scared shit-less at the prospect of an accidental meltdown and being instantly transformed into a quivering pile of guts and bleached bone, all the while taking a hapless teammate or two down with me in the process. Beth's pale, distracted expression bore the same inner fears, as did a few of the others. I'd always heard never waste time worrying about a problem before it actually becomes reality, as most never come to fruition. As things turned out, there were *several* items I shouldn't have birthed a single gray hair fretting over. Commander Virgil would personally man the Flusher Unit-decision finalized by Commander Virgil himself.

As far as the individual teams went (via Virgil once again), Beth and I (dubbed Team 'Alpha' for radio communications purposes) were chosen to descend stairwell number one, with Bohannon and Delbert Prescott (Team 'Bravo') assigned to the second. The third passage, dubbed 'The Hot Zone', was handed to Gaven McCloud, Doc Braggs, and mister team leader himself (Team 'Charlie'). Can't say I felt even the slightest twinge of envy, though I did see Prescott wince a bit at the announcement, while James Bohannon openly groaned. Guess I never was the glory-hound type. Besides, the meeting place for all three teams was eventually gonna be the same, as were the planned treatments. That is, *if* everything went as planned on the way down.

Just as Pretty Boy Garrison stepped up to the stage mike, apparently to regale us with his own personal Knute Rockne-like 'rah-rah' pep rally speech, six black-uniformed, armed-to-the-molars guard-types entered the room and took up position behind both he and the Prof. Each looked to be strapped with both holstered handguns as well as M-16 type rifles, and had donned dark-tinted face-masks with built-in respirators, their identities as big as mystery to us as ours was to them.

Standing at 'parade-rest', they remained diligently silent as the briefing neared conclusion and the witching hour approached. No big issue, that. It wasn't as though any of us were there to socialize. Still, it was a huge relief not to have to worry about dealing with a gang of highly pissed off former project tenants while descending those stone steps towards who the hell knew what.

Despite hard evidence proving otherwise, local media scuttlebutt still hinted that responsibility for both the murders and glut of mysterious disappearances centered on a gang of vigilantes seeking revenge for their forced eviction. In my book, opinions are like a-holes, it's been said, thus personal opinions don't count for much. That said, gut instinct had me leaning heavily towards the bug theory, if for no other reason than the condition of the victims and the aforementioned evidence therein. On the other hand, in terms of prospective dangers, there's little that can match a well-organized team whose hunger and rage is matched only by their thirst for retribution.

Mercifully, Garrison's pre-game talk was shockingly brief, the prologue of which contained an announcement that 'to prove the company's confidence in his hired team's exterminating skills', he'd be leading a site tour later that same afternoon for some visiting investors. As for the epilogue of said speech, it treaded far beyond the simple corn-ball to venture into the outer reaches of pure *hokum*.

"Alright folks, do what you do best. Get down there and kill some goddamned bugs."

Not exactly awe-inspiring in the Rockne 'win one for the Gipper' mode, but at least he'd kept the cornball verbage to a minimum and shied away from patronizing us.

As we filed out of the conference room on the highly-polished heels of our armed escorts, the Prof greeted us with a solemn nod. The last to depart, I returned the gesture. Rain began to fall in thick, rope-like torrents just as our rubber chemical boots hit the outside pavement. Many might've taken this as your textbook 'ominous omen'. Like I've said, I was always above such tripe.

Damn how a man's perspective, not to mention his base beliefs, can change in the time it takes for a single, ear-splitting scream to shellshock his psyche.

"Ahhh yes," Delbert Prescott exclaimed, sounding a tad muffled through the face shield as we simultaneously stepped into the same deceptively deep wading puddle,"it is indeed a good day to exterminate."

Famous *last* words, mister amiable, I recall thinking. Sounds grim, I know, but at that time it was a damn site presumptuous of my cocksure British cohort to assume our roles were that of *predator*.

Regardless, it was time we stepped in with both feet securely planted and all eyes peeled for an enemy yet unidentified. Talk about stumbling blind, it'd be funny if not so fucking tragic. We'd actually thought all the fancy weaponry and accompanying training had been akin to overkill. In truth, *no* amount of prep-time would have sufficed. Literally years of thrice-daily 'war-games' or roll-playing 'real world' scenarios would've made a damned bit of difference in the final outcome.

Seven licensed bug-stompers and six professional soldiers, similarly armed to the teeth. Solid plan…plotted and prepped with every possible stop- gap in case of unforeseen dangers.

137

Sounded secure enough, right? I mean, what could possibly go wrong? *Jesus wept.*

God only knows how one could *truly* be prepared for such hell-bred horrors or for that matter, the reason for their existence.

We didn't have an inkling at the time, but we'd been chosen as renaissance men (and woman) of sorts. Yep-per, we'd be the initial witnesses to the birth of a new era. Sadly, the era being rung in had little plans for mankind as a whole, but then again, mankind as a whole had hardly planned for the colossal shit-storm about to strike.

BUG OUT, PART NINE

Bugging out

No indication of the tragic goat-rope to come, the first half-hour of Operation 'Bug-Out' went as 'smooth as freshly excavated snot', as Beth was apt to say in happier times. Of course, this mainly consisted of last minute equipment and inner-mike checks, team breakdowns and the obligatory 'meet you at the grid' salutes from all involved.

The teams had split almost immediately after suiting up, with Beth and I having the longest trek to our designated passageway at the combination rec room/gymnasium. While ours was a good one-hundred yards from the admin building, AKA 'The Hot Zone', the team of Prescott/Bohannon had trailed off about mid-way towards their target area at the rear of a partially constructed brick structure that was to be a combination community center and meeting hall. Meanwhile, the trio of Commander Virgil, Gaven McCloud and Doc Braggs remained stationed at the admin building, awaiting word whenever the first two teams were past the passages' first checkpoint before beginning their own plunge into the Hot Zone.

While sauntering past mostly hollowed-out, incomplete structures that were no doubt earmarked to be the city's elite high-dollar town-homes, I couldn't help but ponder the fates of all those individuals and family units tossed into the streets to fend for themselves. Pissed off? You bet'cha. Think they'd think twice before linking us with the 'man' and thereby marking us as the 'enemy'? Not a chance. At this point, I trained my sites on our assigned bodyguards and said a silent prayer in behalf of not only our *hides* in general, but that their skills as professional soldiers would remain untested for the duration of the mission.

Once Beth and I entered the stairwell, our silent but stealthy personal bodyguards blazing the well-lit trail, things went from weirdly surreal to downright hairy in no time flat. Thinking back in crystal clear twenty-twenty hindsight, you'd have thought one of us would've noted the conspicuous absence of insect life in and around the sub-division. Probably would've seemed trivial at the time, but as the big picture puzzle fell into place it made perfect sense-tragically so.

First off, there was the initial batch of husks scattered about the bottom three stairs just as we approached locked door number one. The guards tiptoed away from 'em like they were unexploded ordinance, backing against the sentry door like a pair of armed bookends.

More than a decade in the business, and I have to admit to not having a blessed clue what the damn things were, at least not until Beth pointed out a few familiar markings.

"Blowflies, dude," she blurted aloud, no doubt overcompensating for the face shield. She'd cupped several of the larger husks in her left palm, "Biggest damn carcasses I've ever seen."

"You're not kidding, sister," I managed between nervous gulps while kneeling down to investigate a grouping near my left boot,"these bad-

140

boys have been doing some heavy-duty chowing down. Not sure I really wanna know on *what* specifically."

Beth held up King Bloat between her thumb and forefinger, a fly husk roughly the size of a badly warped golf-ball.

"I hear you, boss. Well, whatever the source, it's gotta besomewhere nearby. Guess this joint isn't as air-tight as advertised."

The guards exchanged a look, though it was impossible to gauge their respective expressions through the pitch-black visors. They seemed to be waiting on our permission on whether or not to proceed through the initial blockade. Tossing the bug husks aside, Beth and I first stood and then nodded as one.

Five ticks of the clock and one tapped-out numerical code later, the door slid back with a resounding hum. Following their methodical lead once again, it was obvious the stairwell leading down to door number two was wider, the walls spaced a bit farther apart.

Around step number twenty or so, we watched the guards slowly separate in 'red sea' fashion, each stepping to the side as to allow our immediate approach to whatever had caught their attention.

As Beth was once again the first to spot and/or identify the source of interest, hers was also the initial verbal reaction.

"Holllleee mac-eee-reeeall, boss-man. Check it out."

Secretly, I hated when she called me that. Such a title instantly meant I assumed the leadership role by proxy between the two of us. Just once I'd like to beat her to the punch just to watch those gorgeous eyes widen in shock.

Reaching down, she scooped up and raised the object in a single, fluid movement. Girl always managed a measure of physical grace, no matter the level of hardware that threatened to weigh her down.

"And the winner is. . ," I said, tilting my head a bit as to get a clearer look through the plexi-glass shield as the object swung back and forth like a hypnotist's coin on a chain.

"You tell me, oh master entomologist," she replied with just a hint of uneasiness, pulling the mangled husk closer to her own face,"cause this girl ain't got a blessed clue."

Pinching it between my own gloved fingers, I spun it around several times as to check every available angle while forced to peek around a spattering of fogged-over areas on my face-shield.

"Beetle family is obvious."

I heard Beth's smirk without ever checking the accompanying expression.

"Well no shit, Sherlock Honeybee. Even I knew that much…"

"Could be dung, but the hind legs and elongated pincers don't match the textbook description."

"Damned hybrid of some sort?" Nodding, I tossed the long-dead husk aside and watched it shatter like peanut brittle against the stone flooring alongside at least two dozen similar carcasses.

142

"These days, anything's possible. Question is...how exactly do blowflies and mutated beetles fit into the present storyline?"

Pushing herself upright, Beth reached over with a booted foot and casually scooted our latest find aside, causing the guard closest to her to openly flinch back in response.

"Whoa, dude. No need to panic, at least not just yet," she cracked after a series of what I could only describe as 'dastardly giggles' that the mask had mercifully muffled.

I heard the second guard sigh heavily as he turned to face the small keypad mounted just to the left of the locked door.

"So what's next, chief? A tidal wave of fire ants perhaps? How's about a swarm of highly pissed red-striped scorpions or a similarly stirred up hive of Black-Stinger hornets? Man, so far alllll bets are officially off."

"Stow that kind of talk, woman. Damn it, you're scaring the men," I replied in my best mock superior tone.

Just as the second guard stepped back and the door slid ajar, the first turned directly towards me, snapping his boot-heels together like one of those robotic SS Troops from an ancient WWII war-flick.

"Shouldn't you radio the team leader with these...findings, sir?" I heard Beth's barely subdued giggle in the background.

"Let's just see what we find behind door number one before panicking."

Translation: *what the hell good would it do?* From what I'd seen and heard of one Virgil Hobbs

143

thus far, informing him of said bug husks would likely halt the mission dead in its collective tracks until he could inspect them 'personally'. In other words, more time standing around with our thumbs parked in our hinnies and less solving the mystery at hand. Nope, we'd definitely wait for a more substantial find before contacting the good commander. I didn't even have to ask Bethy's opinion on the matter; the aforementioned snicker had told me all I needed to know.

Bringing up the rear as we shuffled through the newest open space, I was hoping we'd steer clear of any further 'surprises' along the long, winding passage towards the power grid. Wishful thinking that, as the old saying 'you ain't seen nothing yet' had never been so damned appropriate.

We hadn't descended two dozen steps when the guards parted to opposite sides of the stairwell once again, a stiff, mechanical side-step that was becoming damned irritating.

"Oh, what the hell now?" I whispered, the hot bile filing my throat a chunky, rancid mix of the continental breakfast from earlier that morning.

As before, Beth had beaten me to the latest discovery, kneeling down between the guards as if prepping to pray at some unseen Alter.

This time, however, there was no playful banter from the Queen of Barbs; no sarcastic, smart-ass comic one-liners from the Princess of ill-timed quips.

Nope, this time there was nada in the way of smirks, rolled-back eyes or exaggerated hand gestures. This time, there was nothing but a stilted silence that could only mean one thing; shit-creek was backing up and the dam holding back the rising flood of excrement was crumbling but fast.

"Ho-kay, so what's the deal, Lucille…" I began, falling to one knee but still forced to peek over her slumped left shoulder to see what all the new fuss was about.

"You tell me, boss, but whatever…*it* is…I'm not about to touch it."

Scooting over to get an unobstructed look-see, I quickly found myself fighting a strong, instinctual urge to hop up and back against the nearest wall. As it was, I guess the natural curiosity that all fools possess got the better of me.

Both Beth and I were then welding our Tempo Spears like combination chalk-board pointers/batons, balancing them over the pulsating object as if to weld off a possible lunge.

"Almost looks like…but shit, that can't be…" I babbled just as a pair of intertwined shadows loomed overhead. The guards had stepped up behind us, craning forward like interstate rubber-neckers attempting to catch a glimpse of a particularly horrid auto accident.

As my own vocabulary had suddenly gone bone dry in terms of useful production, Beth mercifully followed up on my incomplete gibberish.

"Exactly what I was thinking, boss. It just can't be."

"What…is that thing?" Guard One asked as I heard his boots slide forward another half-step, while Guard Two did just the opposite, actually backing away a similar distance.

"Not a blessed clue," was the only honest response I could manage while watching the end of Beth's spear creep ever closer to the object of our mutual amazement.

"Hey, you're the specialists here," Guard One grumbled, having leaned so close I could feel a slight pressure on my upper back from his extended knee.

"We don't claim to be entomologists, buddy-boy," Beth finally retorted with a sarcastic grit that instantly helped settle my nerves somewhat.

"We don't stash 'em in Mason jars and study 'em. We just kill 'em.

Personally, my best guess on this downright *repulsive* SOB would fall somewhere in-between animal, mineral, or possibly fucking alien in nature. You concur, boss-man?"

For the second time in less than two minutes, I was struck utterly speechless; the gist of my concentration focused on the enigmatic monstrosity posed eight to ten inches from the tip of my right boot.

It was one of those moments in life, however rare, that surely justified the well-worn phrase '*you had to see to believe it.* ' Even with all the new and as-of- yet uncategorized species of insect popping up in the past several years, this went beyond simple hybrid-types or generic sub-species. As Beth has so eloquently put it, the question of whether to label this thing insect, animal, or perhaps 'other' was a total crapshoot from a visual standpoint. Beth had hit one other detail squarely on the head as well. Be it mammal, amphibian, insect or Hollywood horror flick special effect come to life, it was just about the *ugliest* damn thing I'd ever laid eyes on. Approximately the size of an adult mole, it looked to be part maggot and part praying mantis, with just a hint of granddaddy long-legs tossed in for mutated measure.

"Is it...is it dead?" Guard Two asked from a distance, not to mention a bit too timidly for a man being paid to 'protect and serve' our collective hides.

"Hardly think so, Ace...unless we've unearthed a race of *zombie*-bugs,' Beth responded, having practically laid the tip of the spear atop the thing's octagon-shaped noggin, 'cause it seems to be chowing down to beat the band. Yeech,...you *seeing* this, boss?"

Though I was faintly aware of Beth's inquiry, the creature's spastic feeding movements had me partially entranced, not to mention the target of its hunger.

"Earth to Jack...come in, Jack..."

"Oh, sorry...it's just that...what'd you say?"

"Just wondering if you might identify said creepy-crawly, or perhaps even the main course it seems to be gorging itself on at the moment," she repeated, gently tapping the thing's spiny back with the spear-tip.

Taking in a lungful, I couldn't help but wonder what fascinating yet frightening wonders might still await us behind door number three. Not ashamed to say a rather large portion of my inner-subconscious favored flight with a big ol' bolded capitol 'F'.

"No idea on the feeder, but it isn't much of a stretch on what's left of the mystery meat. In taking Anatomy one-oh-one for a thousand, Alex, I'd definitely say femur bone."

"As in…*human* femur?" Guard Two asked, his tone having dropped several octaves to near pre-teen stage. At the same time, Beth yanked that spear away like exposed fingers from a lit burner. The thing seemed oblivious to our presence as it continued to feed, its bloated body throbbing like gestating larvae. It held each particle of meat in hooked pinchers, hence the praying mantis similarity, while its miniscule jaws tore and chomped with ravenous glee.

"You're saying the flesh and sinew that thing's vacuuming off is of…human origin? But…how can you be sure?"

"He's right," Guard One chimed in while once again kneeing me in the upper back,"I spent two years as an EMT…that's a large one…more than likely a good-sized male."

"Think…it's um…time to contact the others now, Mister Barton?"

Using my own spear as a crutch, I stood at parade-rest without ever daring to take my eyes off the grisly prize.

"Yeah, this is one find Virgil and the gang might want to see for themselves."

As instructed, I reached up towards my face-mask and located the tiny transmit button just below my chin.

"Let's just hope the crazy bastard doesn't ask us to 'bag it' for further study," Beth said with a strained grin, while hopping up to stand to my immediate left.

"Long as it's a dead *or* alive proposition, dead being the preferred choice," I answered just before a loud static crack filled my ears. Talk about your twentieth century technology surviving well into the twenty-first, blasted thing worked like your basic walkie-talkie. Press to speak, let off to receive. You didn't know whether to bend over in hysterics or break down and cry. All the money at New Horizons disposal and we were forced to communicate like pre-teens in a neighborhood tree-house.

"Virgil, um…Team Charlie, this is Team Alpha, over…"

In the thirty to forty-five seconds of silence and occasional static that followed, I watched Beth roll her eyes in disgust before turning to the guards with an exaggerated shrug.

"Guess Virgil figured the bugs might intercept our radio transmission. I mean, gee whiz fellas, we can't have a nest of giant assassin bugs finding out our 'secret identities', now can we? Born leader, that dude," she concluded with a mock salute.

"Go ahead, Alpha…" Virgil finally responded, the booming volume of which threatened to pop both my eardrums. I wasn't sure if the problem was technical or perhaps our fearless yet excitable leader bellowing into the mike at full bore. Regardless, my reply was not of the slightly annoyed but highly pissed off nature.

"Holy sh-…um, tone it down if at all possible, Virg…uh, Charlie. You damn near shattered my face shield, over."

"Not of my doing, Alpha…wireless glitch of some type. State your business, over…"

Whatever the com gremlin's origin, Virgil must've whispered the second go-round, as the decibel level had been at least two-fold milder.

"Much better, Charlie. Just wanted to pass on a rather…unique finding here in stairwell two. Kind of…hard to describe but involves…bug species of new origin, over."

"Damn, but you're a natural-born communicator," Beth cracked with a wink, to which I playfully flashed a double-fisted bird her way.

"We've run into a similar…um…unidentifiable enigma here, Alpha, also while ascending the stairs leading into the grid.

Prescott…um…team Bravo reported the same just moments ago. Over."

While combing through the cobwebs for a suitable reply slash query, I peered over at Beth with what must've been one whopper of a confused expression, as she burst into a fit of uncontrolled hysterics.

"Did heap big boss-man actually just say *enema*?" she finally asked, and I saw the fresh tears flow down each of her rose-shaded cheeks.

"Be advised, Charlie. The mystery species we've encountered is currently…feeding on what appears to be a bone of human origin. Over."

150

I heard one or possibly both of Honor Guard Security's finest release a strained sigh, as if impatiently awaiting the order to abort mission.

"Understood, Alpha. Team Bravo report numerous bone fragments near their grid entrance, while the very walls near our entrance here are coated in what appears to be blood smears and shreds of discarded tissue. Over."

Following a solid half-minute of silence, Beth shrugged in open frustration as all eyes turned towards the still-feeding entity. Amazing, but the damned thing hadn't been at all phased by either our unexpected arrival or continued noisy presence.

"Sooooooo…what's it gonna be, Virgil?" I finally blurted, feeling my gorge re-arise at the sight of bleached bone being systemically nibbled squeaky clean,"do we just keep on trekking or collect samples and head back up top to regroup?"

"Give me a moment while I re-contact Bravo on their situation…"

It was a distinctly different voice that broke the silence some ten to fifteen seconds later.

"Butt-ugly little bastards, aren't they? Roger Dodger and Over."

Beth's face instantly brightened at hearing McCloud's ultra-cheery voice, as did my very spirit. The man simply had that effect.

"You got that right, Gaven. Ever see anything like it? Over…"

"Not unless you count shitty CGI from some cheapie Sci-Fi flick. What blows my mind is the menu these things seem to favor. Over…"

151

"Creep city, alright. Is Bravo…are Prescott and Bohannon dealing with the same species? Over."

"Sounds like it. Equal parts maggot and mantis, with an outer casing that reminds me of the armadillo's I used to run across while drivin' through the panhandle. Over."

"Ours is the size of a hamster. Over."

"Feel fortunate, my man. We're starin' down triplets here, all of 'em kitten sized but with Saint Bernard appetites. Over."

I was about to inquire specifics concerning his 'menu' comment when Beth broke in with a question of her own.

"Are…do they seem aggressive towards you or just…damned apathetic? Over."

"Seems to me they don't give a good rat's behind whether we're here or not. Over."

"Same here," I injected as Beth turned back to the thing and kneeled before it, though with a marked cautiousness that had been conspicuously absent just minutes before. I surely couldn't blame her for falling prey to a sudden case of frazzled nerves. Just watching the thing stuff its face with dead human tissue while simultaneously studying us with those cold, pit-black, weirdly reptilian eyes had every fiber of hair on my body standing fully erect and moistened with freshly birthed sweat.

"Scariest thing is the way it just ignores u-. ."

"Enough chatter, people," Virgil interrupted in his trademark tone, that being persistently perturbed with just a subtle hint of cockiness.

"Alright…here's the deal: before entering the grid room, each team leader will utilize his B&G

sprayer and saturate the…unidentified bug-species so we might get an idea of exactly what we're dealing with here. Copy that, team leaders?"

Beth and I exchanged an awkward glance, and I didn't dare response 'til she gave me the high sign.

"Guess he means you, boss," she succumbed with her patented 'who cares?' shrug, though deep down I knew the omission, no doubt due solely to her sex, frosted her no end. Thick-skinned as she'd become through the years, it was still quite the pisser.

"Affirmative, Alpha. Charlie team copies…will saturate and evaluate. Over."

"Bravo team copies, Alpha. Will do same and subsequently advise. Over," Prescott replied in a cockney tongue so thick I could've sworn he'd been possessed by the spirit of the late Sir Sean Connery.

"Copy that, Charlie and Bravo. That Demon/BP mix should liquefy said pest in a matter of thirty-seconds or less. Keep me posted, men. Over."

"Keep me posted, *men*," Beth spat through a deep frown,"chauvinistic jackass…remember to sacrifice the woman and children first, mate ties! Toss 'em to the sharks and then we'll down a few frosty ones while taking turns scratching each others groins and measuring the respective boners before the nightly nose- pickin' contest!" Miraculously, the two guards managed to remain unaffected even as I damn near fell to my knees in hysterics. Maybe it was their paramilitary training, the brainwashing effects of which strictly prohibited spontaneous outburst of jocularity; perhaps my partner's stone-faced, acid-tongued rant simply didn't strike them as funny; or maybe it was simply a matter of both possessing a sense of humor equivalent to your basic houseplant. Regardless, I was beyond caring for the thirty to forty-five second span that my lungs locked up like cheap brakes and freshly spurted tears threatened to fill my mask up the eyebrows. I was only around sixty-percent recouped when Bethy stepped up and landed a stout elbow into my ribs, thereby hasting my recovery.

"You 'bout done, boss? What say we douse that repulsive little shit and enjoy the body-melt aftermath?"

"I'm with you, woman. Now, if you don't mind, hand me that sprayer while I scratch my groins."

A slick, cool to the touch metal wand slapped my exposed palm a few ticks later, and I took several baby-steps forward as Beth pumped the B&G to a high pressure setting. May sound chicken-shit, but the old pulse rate went off the charts as I pointed the nozzle and prepped to fire. All things considered, that damned mutation should've been blasted airborne, being that firing distance was less than two feet and the sprayer was set at maximum pressure. As it was, it hardly budged a blessed iota, though its meal was ripped from its grip and tossed against the grid entrance with a sharp, wet thumping sound. Just seconds before that lethal dosage of Demon/BP-400 began its dirty work, I caught a brief peek at why the thing had stuck to the floor as if nailed down. Dozens of tiny suction cubs on its underbelly, much like those of octopi or squid.

154

"Beth, you seeing this?"

Joining me in keeping at least a semi-safe distance as the thing's bloated torso began to gradually melt away, I hadn't even realized Beth had gently retrieved the wand from my right hand and reattached to the B&G.

"Affirmative, boss. Maybe it's the universe's first aqua/bug hybrid. Who knows, maybe it was one of those rare full-moon orgies between maggot, mantis, and sea horse."

Despite the wisecracks, all traces of good humor had faded from my partners tone as we watched the object of our apprehension transformed to bubbling black goop in a matter of minutes. At that point, logic dictated relief as the emotion that should've ruled the day. After all, one of the lesser weapons in our vast arsenal had performed above and beyond the call. This definitely seemed to bode well in terms of future eradicating success, no matter the level of genetic horror that lay ahead.

Instead, what was left in the aftermath of the kill brought forth a wave of solid fear and foreboding that caused my poor old ticker to skip a beat or two.

"Jesus Crow, Jack-O, check it out. Correct me if I'm wrong...but it...it looks like a...like some kinda..."

"Exo-skeletal mass," I concluded for Beth, whose rapid breathing and jittery movements were a sure sign of what I oft referred to as her 'red-line burnout' stage, wherein she'd work herself into a nerve-wracking frenzy before the eventual unraveling in both a mental a physical sense. I had

155

to do my best to nip this in the bud, less I'd essentially find myself performing a solo once inside the grid area.

"But then, we both, we allll know that insects, as a general rule, do not possess bone structure as we know it, correct?"

"Holy shit, it is…I mean, it does. Looks like bones, I mean," Guard One babbled, leaning between us like a curious bystander at a particularly grisly crash scene.

The slick, prickly remains were poised like a feeding mantis, each pincher still locked in full grip mode. Its hind end, a spiny tail that appeared more reptilian than anything from the insect world, whipped back and forth several times before finally sliding to a final halt. Retrieving my spear, I used its tip as a pointer and gently tapped the skeleton from the front end, though careful not to tip it over. Not exactly sure why I wanted to keep it intact-treating it as some sort of exotic and priceless museum piece-definitely weird behavior for one paid to extract destruction on such entities.

"All joking aside, I'm beginning to think what we're dealing with here *is* more animal than insect."

"Check out the beak, Jack. With that armored face-plate stripped away, it's a dead ringer for an Assassin bug."

As usual in the ID and description department, she was right on. A natural-she could've made one hell of an entomologist.

"It surely does," I agreed, placing the spear-tip flush against the slightly hooked appendage in question,"that's one big-ass beak alright. Probably

156

sucks out tissue like an industrial-strength Hoover. Gotta give King Virgil credit for knowing just what pesticide mix to melt 'em down with."

"You'd better…um, might want to inform him…uh…your boss of this…um…new development," Guard Two managed to stammer, his back so tightly entrenched against a far wall it was as if he were literally trying to scale his way up towards the ceiling.

He was right, of course, though it was a safe bet that such a startling 'find' would be old news to the other teams by then.

Speculation became fact just seconds later, as both Alpha and Bravo confirmed both similar meltdowns and aftermath-related remains. By the time Virgil got on the horn and issued his next group order, the gnawing fear at the center of my gut had long passed its initial and middle stages and was shooting for full-blown panic status. For Bethy's sake more than my own, I knew better than to even hint at such feelings.

"All teams will hereby proceed to the grid with B&G's at the ready, settings at highest pressure. Also ensure each team member has easy access to an Intruder grenade and turbo rifles. Security officers please take up guarded positions outside the grid entrance and await extermination teams' eventual exit. Everyone read? Over."

"Team Bravo reads loud and clear. Proceeding onward, over," Prescott replied, as disgusted cheery as ever, though I seriously doubted his muscle-bound partner shared such enthusiasm.

"Team Charlie, ditto. Over."

"Okay people, let's be on our toes in there. If we're looking down the barrel at a nesting of these things, its libel to get read spicy real fast. Just soak 'em, bomb 'em and move on. Remember, we're here to eradicate the pest, no matter the identity. Over and out."

"General Patton he ain't," Beth quipped, pumping her turbo sprayer to the max as I re-checked my own.

"Must be one of those 'lead by example' guys, you think?"

"Partner, let's hope we never have to find out if and when the mythical excrement hits the fan," I replied, making certain an aforementioned grenade was duly secured to my utility belt and thereby easily reached for quick detachment. I watched Beth remove and then re-attach her own poison-filled pineapple before she turned to me and struck a mock 'at attention' pose.

"Amen to that, brother. You watch my backside...I'll watch yours."

"Always a pleasure to do so, my dear," I blurted through possibly the most insincere smile I'd manufactured in years, although truer words had never been spoken. All ex-lovers considered, Beth Cambridge had the shapeliest caboose I'd ever had the pleasure to gawk at/and or service.

"Buns of steel...ah yes...butt-cheeks constructed of the finest titanium."

Matching my faux grin with a jaw-stretcher of her own, Beth firmly slapped my lone exposed shoulder and we whirled about as one to face the entry door.

"Might as well open 'er up, guys. We're as ready as we'll ever be." Lord God, or so I thought at the time.

As earlier mentioned, there are indeed those rare occasions when prep time, however lengthy, is reduced to a useless formality; a trivial time-waster with no effect whatsoever on a scenario's eventual outcome. Unfortunately, a hand-picked group of so-called extermination professionals were about to experience such an occasion, up close and personal.

BUG OUT, PART TEN

Breaking out in Hives

"Hey, at least the powers still up. Thought for a sec we were gonna have to break out the old pen-lights," Beth exclaimed as we stepped side-by-side through the surprisingly well-lit entrance.

"My lady, if that had been the case, you would've bore witness to the most graceful, technically proficient 'about face' maneuver in the annuals of recorded history."

Check out the paint job. You'd think we were in some fancy hotel lobby."

As opposed to the previous stairwell's bland green coating, the interior walls of the lowest level were plastered in a dark brown hue with a foot-thick yellow stripe running the length at around waist level.

"Makes about as much sense as the general layout-damned architect must've been on crack," Beth replied as we both took a second to recheck our weaponry.

We heard the entrance door clang shut behind us, a booming echo that aided in the rebirth of several thousand chill-bumps all along my outer shell.

We'd both slung around in haste, Beth even accidentally coating the inner door with a stout spray of pesticide.

"And then there were but two…"

"Um, boss…"

"The tomb of death, this underground concrete mausoleum, would be their final stomping grounds…"

"Geez boss. . ."

"And they were never seen or heard from again…"

"You can cut it out now, Jack. Shit ain't the least bit humorous," Beth snapped as we turned to face the fresh, virgin terrain ahead. Bad as I hate to go the cliché route, I'd never truly experienced a healthier dose of foreboding- standing in that twisting, curving, stone-encased hallway that led to who the hell knew what. For several ticks of the clock, I reverted back to preschool age: Unsure, disoriented, and scared completely out of my wits. As usual, it was my icy-veined partner that snapped me back, her rapier wit the equivalent of a sharp slap to the face.

"C'mon, Jack-O. Let's find the others and commence soaking this joint 'til it's raining ugly little beasties screaming for their very lives…" she raised a finger in protest,"…but to no fucking avail."

No doubt resembling futuristic storm-troopers, we trudged forward, though personally with great reservations. The lone comforting thought was that of reuniting with the other teams. I'd always heard the term 'strength in numbers'. Seemed like the perfect scenario to test such a theory.

Unlike the other two stairwells, level three was an altogether different animal in terms of both distance and visual limitations. Upon entry one was faced with an unusually spacious foyer area, though logic escapes as to why the boxed-shaped room was allowed extra space to house exactly nothing but a nearby metal sign proclaiming *'DANGER: RESTRICTED AREA – LINE BADGE CHECKPOINT AHEAD'*.

Beth ran a gloved palm across the sign as if checking it for dust. "Must've had a regular guard shack set-up down here at one point. No reason to speculate why it was discarded."

"Safe bet. New Horizons my ass. From what we've been told they ought to rename the whole damn subdivision 'Bermuda Triangle' east."

"You tell 'em, Chief. I just love it when you talk dirty."

Rounding that first lengthy curve had a dizzying effect; no doubt aided by the fluorescent yellow striping that seemed to visibly widen the further we walked. Optical illusion I'm sure, though still irritating as hell. It didn't help matters that the 'echo' effect seemed to intensify ten-fold at the lowest level, the end result being Beth and I sounded like a couple of 'one-man' bands with all the clunky gear we were forced to haul.

The curve eventually petered out at a railed stairwell of perhaps twenty steps, the bright blue walls and yellow stripe quickly replaced by regulation puke green as we descended. Trekking along a noticeably narrower corridor towards a second stairwell, I could feel my chest begin to tighten. Wasn't sure at the time if it was stress or exertion-related. One thing's a certainty: The B&G seemed to weigh a far site more than its max-filled weight of twenty-five pounds. My legs were lead:

my biceps, forearms, and hands trembling; my shoulders burning like red-hot coals. I was glad Beth had taken point, as I was sure she'd eventually notice my gait growing increasingly wobbly. Though neither of us had dared breach the subject as of yet, it was strange how we hadn't spotted a single bug, husk or otherwise, since entering the lowest level. No evidence of insect or any other form of life, for that matter. Nary a carcass; much less of the running variety. More than once I was tempted to halt our progress to give Virgil and the others a quick buzz, mostly out of blatant curiosity but also just to hear a voice other than the annoying coward jabbering away within my own subconscious.

Stairwell number two was roughly half the length of the first, and we were soon halted dead in our collective tracks facing still another brightly lit warning sign, this particular one attached to a seven to eight foot high chain-link fence and lit up in tri-color neon, reading:

'AUTHORIZED PERSONNEL ONLY: ELECTRICAL ROOM. TRESSPASSERS WILL BE DETAINED AND DULY CHARGED'.

"Sounds like they mean it, boss," Beth cracked as we both readjusted our spray units, carefully set them aside and paused for a much-needed breather.

"No doubt a result of all the recent vandalism. Well, I'd say we qualify as Authorized. Shall we press on, my lady?"

"Only if we desire the rather hefty paycheck to follow, my *man*."

"I'll take the lead then."

With a slight bow, Beth waived me on. Brave and determined, not to mention *greedy*, soldiers that we were, we scooped up our respective sprayers and traipsed forward.

After passing through the fenced-in gates, which had been mysteriously left wide open with the entrance doors pulled ajar, we passed a series of large generator units from which snaked anaconda-sized cords leading to what I perceived to be the main grid.

"This place is huge, boss. Where's the blessed finish line already?" Beth whined as she switched arms lugging the B&G for at least the third time since we'd hit lower level.

"Hold up, Beth," I countered, slowing my steps as we grew near still another sharp turn to the right,"let me buzz Virgil and make sure we're all headed in the same direction for this little pow-wow."

"Kick it in high gear, boss...I'm blazing the old trail," she countered, the over-stuffed backpack between her narrow shoulder blades shifting about like a live entity. Allowing my B&G to fall to one side, I reached up and found the magic 'speak' button once again.

"Virgil...damn! Alpha, this is Brav-...shit! This is Charlie team...t-team Charlie...we're deep inside level three-just passed through a fenced in zone marked electrical room. Do you read? Over."

Static. . . followed by even more static, interrupted only sporadically by a low hissing sound not unlike a punctured tire leaking its contents ever-so- gradually.

"Alpha...do you read? Bravo team, do *you* read?"

As before, nothing...nada...zilch...at least in terms of an actual verbal response. I could only fathom we, being the teams, we're too damn close in terms of proximity, thus somehow shorting out com capability. Never claimed to be an expert in such matters-obviously for good reason. Meantime, despite my plea, Beth had vanished behind a Mack-truck sized computer hub approximately twenty to twenty-five yards from where I stood.

"Dammit Virgil, do...you. . . read? McCloud? Prescott, you guys down here or did we take a wrong turn somewhere outside Albuquerque? Hel-lo?

Helll.... llloooow? Echo. . . echo. . ." It seems whenever I'm on the verge of complete panic, I revert back to my 'Looney-Tunes' upbringing.

This time, the incessant hissing went solo for a full thirty seconds before the com lines seemed to go completely dead. Cradling my B&G like a metallic lifesaver, I took off in a shambling jog, tracing Beth's steps on legs fast transforming into semi-flaccid rubber.

Just past the giant, gray-colored hub, the whole place got real dark real damn fast. I'm talking *hand in front of your face and barely able to make out the wriggling fingers* dark.

At this point I skidded to a clumsy stop, thus beginning a rather embarrassing three to four step transformation into my alter-ego during such stressful times-a being that bore a strange resemblance to any and all of the Three Stooges. Step one-the B&G canister flew from my grip, rolling noisily into the darkness as I groped thin air with both hands. Step two-the aforementioned groping session, teamed with a forward momentum issue that tangled my ankles as if literally roped and tied, sent me sprawling face-first onto cool, damp flooring. Step three-rolling hard to my left, I both felt and heard a simultaneous snapping directly between my shoulder blades.

"Super-duper, Jack my boy. Here's hoping that handy-dandy turbo rifle won't be needed later on, 'cause it's gonna be damn hard to fire through a shattered barrel."

Pulling the broken barrel free from its torn leather holster, I tossed it into the darkness and scrambled to my feet.

"Beth…can you hear me? Beth?"

Hard as it was to believe, I was huffing and puffing like a marathon runner within a stone's toss of the finish line.

"Beth, are you in here? Jesus, somebody find the light-switch already." Now past the point of simple uneasiness, I was walking that thin line between extreme apprehension and scared freaking shit-less.

"Damn it girl…where the hell are you?"

Running my hands about that skin-tight uniform like a rapist groping his latest victim in a

166

blackened alleyway, I eventually fell upon the twelve-volt flashlight strapped onto the far left side of my utility belt.

"While I'm on the subject, where the hell is *anybody*? Awww, for shits sake…"

Holding the light in a badly shaking right hand, I managed to find the power-up and instantly flinched back from the explosion of light the surprisingly wide beam produced.

"Shiiiit, let there be light indeed."

Once my temporary blindness subsided, I froze into place like a man standing at the center of a live minefield. I'd venture to say the full-body paralysis lasted a good half to full minute; the lone body functions still operable being a pair of wildly flaring nostrils and a badly twitching right eye. I had somehow stumbled directly into a wide, tunnel-shaped chasm-roughly twelve to maybe fifteen feet in total diameter, its rock walls slick with condensation. For a second, a single tick in time, I can't deny thinking about a hasty retreat. It wasn't exactly bravery or even a grave concern for my partner's welfare that quickly dismissed the possibility, but in shining the light in the direction I'd come, it was equally dark and thereby equally as fearsome.

Stupidly, I even attempted to cup my hands around my mouth to shout out, which of course was effectively blocked by the clear visor.

"Ah, the hell with this useless piece of crap anyway," I raged, pulling the headgear apparatus clear with one stout tug and dropping it near my left boot, thus allowing the cup-the-lips technique without further complications.

"Beth!   Beth…Deandra…Cambridge! *BEEEEETTTTH!*" I bellowed to no avail, as the aftermath provided no response other than a ringing echo.

Another trait I'd developed in times of great duress was a noted increase in the use of profanities. With that in mind, both Grandma and Mama Barton would've been plugging their ears in shame for several shell-shocked moments. Chalk it up to nervous habit-guess it beats smoking or gnawing one's fingernails down to the nubs.

"Rest assured, once this colossally fucked-up goat-rope session is history, I'm gonna have somebody's ass…just on general fucking principles alone."

Before proceeding, I re-fitted the mask as to give the com device another chance.

"May Day…I repeat…May fucking Day…this is Jack Barton of team Charlie…does anyone read me?

"Virgil? McCloud? Prescott? Shit. Bohannon? Braggs? Son of a *bitch.*

If anybody can hear me, I'm presently headed down the tunnel of love in pursuit of an old flame. Got it?

Fuck it then…taking inventory and moving on."

Retrieving the B&G canister some fifteen feet ahead-laying on its slightly dented side like a giant-sized soda can-I stepped cautiously within the foot-wide beam the light so effectively sliced into the murk.

I must've covered a good fifteen or twenty yards when the tunnel seemed to grow gradually narrower. At first I considered the 'imagination running wild' possibility-followed quickly by the 'it's just a trick of the light or lack thereof' theory. But, another ten to fifteen steps totally debunked either notion. The tunnel had lost a foot or more in circumference as my boots were forced to close ranks until the kneecaps and ankles would periodically brush together.

"Beth, can you hear me? BETH!" I screamed, the effort causing the left side of my visor to briefly fog up. With no response apparently eminent, I lumbered on. It wasn't as if my fear had subsided, on the contrary, if anything the building dread constricted ever tighter around my chest cavity with each step. Personal cowardice, for which I possessed in mass abundance, no longer applied. Turning back was simply no longer an option. Whatever I was to encounter, be it man or bug, lay somewhere in the distance ahead. I could only hope I wouldn't be doing a solo when or if said encounter occurred.

For several frantic seconds, I pondered the possibility of the pathway growing increasingly narrow, to the point where I'd be forced to crawl forward on my hands and knees like a tunneling rat. Such panic-fueled worries were soon banished, however, shoved roughly aside by cold, stark reality. My right boot tip had struck an unseen object protruding upward from the tunnel floor, temporarily throwing me off-balance. While attempting to regain a semblance of balance, the flashlight beam wavered and shook in my hand, briefly sailing upward and striking the ceiling several feet above. Falling onto my hands and knees, I paused before ever daring to refocus the light in a vertical pose. The reasoning behind this particular 'break in the action' was three-fold. Reason one was to allow my lungs to properly refill from the sudden jettisoning they'd experienced on the way down. Reason two was purely sanity-related, as I had to take a short sabbatical in order to mentally coerce myself into refocusing the light without fear of completely losing my marbles. This wasn't merely a claustrophobia issue either. The shaky imagery I'd locked on was solely of the nightmarish variety, and I wasn't at all certain a reviewing was a good idea if indeed said images were based in reality.

Hey, it wasn't as if I *hoped* I'd gone bonkers. Insanity should never be considered a healthy state of mind after all. Nuts is nuts, after all, despite the scenario at hand. That said, while propped like a panting canine atop a cold, wet slab inside a pitch-dark tunnel, the last thing this boy wanted to be was right on in terms of what he *thought* he'd seen.

Reason three was curiosity related, as upon landing I'd once again tossed my B&G forward and buried both hands into a mushy, mysterious mound that the light soon revealed as some sort of pliable, honeycomb substance. If nothing else, this left little doubt on what I'd tripped on. The honeycomb appeared to either be dark green or purple, and lined not only the floor but all sides of the tunnel as far ahead as the light could reveal.

"Jesus, carpenter bees maybe?" I mumbled, taking turns whipping each gloved hand about as to disengage the gooey afterbirth from the fingers and palms.

"Can't be. They don't...build hives like...like this. Shit...let's hope this isn't in anyway related to those mutated assassin bugs..."

Just the thought loosened my bowels. Discretion being the larger part of valor, I wasn't about to lay about the nest awaiting the answer. Instead, after once again retrieving the sprayer, this time coated in greenish slime, I made tracks as fast as the soft, sickeningly moist terrain would allow.

Can't say how much ground I actually covered before the dead end halted all forward progress, but it must've upwards of a hundred yards or more.

It had been years since I'd encountered a dirt-dauber's nest, but the wall blocking my way certainly held a similar look, not to mention texture; a hardened outer shell riddled with vertical holes that best resembled Swiss cheese carved from baked clay.

Dropping the sprayer to my side, I placed both palms flat against the wall as to test its overall tinsel strength. It was about the same time I'd concluded it was far less than impenetrable that I was given a hell of a good reason to test said theory. A low humming sound reverberated from the opposite direction; one that was to grow increasingly loud as seconds passed, mutating into a pulsating roar that caused my chest and midsection to shake and

171

vibrate even as my eyeballs grew moist from the impending onslaught. The lone description that fit the phenomenon was, of course, an utter impossibility in a sane world. Then again, I was beginning to wonder if level three weren't a separate universe altogether-a decidedly warped 'Alter-Earth' where grotesque abnormalities were the norm, as I swear that ear-splitting screech sounded like a termite swarm on steroids.

Four good whacks with the B&G began what a half-dozen side-kicks from my left boot finished, creating a circular exit just large enough squeeze my bulk into and belly-crawl through. The first thing I noticed, even while attempting to sling away a thick coat of dirt/goo from my gloves, was the spattering of light filling the mystery room. It was downright surreal, it not a bit hypnotizing, like strobe lights being turned on and off at timed intervals. The club scene of my late teen and early twenties instantly came to mind, though instantly accompanied by a vibe of sheer creepiness. Whatever freak-filled chamber I'd stumbled into, it sure as hell weren't no disco.

At this particular point of the journey, I can honestly state I'd never before so desperately sought human contact. Heaven forbid Beth make a surprise appearance, as my tired old heart might well have exploded from an overdose of joyous glee. Sad to say, believing in such miracles held little in terms of logic. Reality was truly a bitch, no matter how hopelessly warped or skewed by practical improbabilities.

Getting to my feet, I performed the initial walk-around with the speed of a three-toed sloth with a slashed Achilles heel (shit, do Sloth's even have those?). As visibility was limited to those two to three second gaps when the lights shone, it took a few moments to get a firm grasp on such details as room size, shape, and finally, the contents contained within.

As things shook out, that third item could've remained unanswered for all I cared.

The shape was squared, almost perfectly so, the four walls made up of the same box-shaped hives. Size-wise, I'd have guess-ti-mated it perhaps twenty yards wide and thirty to thirty-five in overall length, though the lunatic- fringe lighting reduced this to a far less than scientific conclusion.

As far as the aforementioned contents, I strolled about in a continuous circle for several minutes, having utilized my flashlight for validation purposes. This only after discovering the uniquely bizarre source of lighting- four live Lampyridae had been separately mounted in each corner by some type of constructive webbing. As kids growing up in the Midwest we called 'em 'Lightning Bugs' and caught and placed 'em in jelly jars for an instant candle- effect. Only thing was, these particular ones were the size of your basic housecat, each powerful pulsation revealing a completely hollowed-out abdomen.

Alas, what I'd discover next made the giant fireflies appear positively mundane by comparison.

A massive pile of bones, most of which appeared human though some were obviously canine in origin, centered the room and were piled three to four feet high. Even viewed through amateur eyes, the skull and rib cages were the easiest to ID, as were smaller skeletal formations that were surely of the pet variety. Despite their many differences, all had one specific thing in common; they'd been stripped meticulously clean and appeared almost bleached-snow white ivories glistening in a coating of the same syrupy mix that I'd sunk my gloves into upon submerging them into the honeycomb nesting within the tunnel. The connection between these and the striped femurs of level two wasn't at all clear, just as it seemed a bit premature to pin the blame on those mutated mantis bugs, but it was damned apparent that *coincidence* held little validity. Funny, it didn't occur to me right away that such a massive collection of remains held absolutely no odor to speak of. I had begun to suspect that the majority of my senses had been systemically cancelled out by the element of shock. Despite the building lunacy, a part of me still feared for Beth at a level much greater than myself, though not so much for the others. No guilt there…I hardly knew 'em, after all. Bethy on the other hand…well, there's a lot to be said for friendship and loyalty…not all of it mushy or cornball in the least.

Exactly how long the grisly scene entranced both mind and body is a mystery, the self-imposed daze finally broken by an ever greater jolt of horror. Though I'd walked the room's perimeter just moments earlier, only now did the shapes swim into view, first to be visualized from the corner of my left eye.

Wasn't sure if they were a new addition to the building funhouse or a detail I'd somehow, incredible as it seemed, missed altogether the first time around. Odds being what they were, I had to concede to the former, least accept the slow but inevitable dissipation of my own sanity. Thick strands of webbing had apparently dropped from the honeycombed ceiling as I'd been so acutely mesmerized. I counted five in all, each as thick as nautical cord rope, swinging back and forth like knotty pendulums and pulled taut and visibly straining to hold their bulky cargo airborne.

"Oh for cripes…who wrote this script, Richard *Fucking* Matheson?" I screeched aloud, the reference of course to the great twentieth century Sci-Fi scribe of such masterpieces as 'The Incredible Shrinking Man' and 'The Last Man on Earth', also noteworthy as a personal favorite of mine.

For all apparent purposes, they appeared to be larvae pods of the insect variety on the verge of hatching. My curiosity having long given way to base cowardice, I wasn't about to hang around for the birthing. Backing ever- cautiously towards the tunnel entrance, I held the B&G in one arm while gripping an intruder grenade in the other. In retrospect, perhaps my purposely slow exit wasn't entirely vigilance-related but equally driven by a morbid fascination-the possibility of catching a peek at a phenomenon never before viewed by man. It's only natural, after all. Man's penchant for searching out the weird and surreal is well-noted throughout history, otherwise the majority of the great 'discoveries' of modern times might've given way to many a soiled undergarment.

Besides, by this point the whole thing seemed less real than a walking nightmare, thus the element of fear had diminished in lieu of a stout sense of disbelief. Bottom line: I wasn't buying all the wacky shit I was supposedly seeing anyhow…might as well see it through to whatever conclusion my warped imagination could create. I'd been a big reader of comics and graphic novels as a kid. As for the origin of such a spaced-out mind-bender of a hallucination. . . maybe I'd fallen down one of the stairwells and cracked my noggin or accidentally set off one of the intruder grenades and thus self-poisoned myself into a chemical-induced coma. On the other hand, there is a sense of comfort in believing no harm can befall one in a dream. Regardless, I had one foot planted inside the tunnel before freezing into place. It was about that same time that the hanging pods began to shake and shimmy; gently at first and then with increased fervor until they resembled overstuffed eggplants blown about by gale-force winds. It was also about this same time that a few mind-marbles shifted out of position and I began to babble and rant as a way, I suppose, to work off a shit- load of nervous energy.

"*BETH! VIRGIL! DOC*! Anybody else seeing this crazy shit? *HELLLLL- LOOOOO*! All I can say is…you're all missing one hell of a show here!

Don't be shy, dammit! Feel free to join in if the urge arises…just make sure you enter locked and/or loaded, 'cause whomever the host may be, they don't seem very hospitable, at least on the surface…*HELLLLLL-FUCKING-LOOOOOOOOOOOOO!*"

Without evening knowing it, I'd began to saturate the nearest pod with a constant spray from the B&G, the micro-injector having been pre-set at its highest pressure setting.

While the other four cocoon larvae continued to spasm and wriggle with increased fervor, the one I'd coated with enough Demon-X to wipe out a dozen colonies of Jamaican Flesh-Eaters had ceased all movement. Jerking my trigger finger free and aiming the nozzle elsewhere, I soon found myself backed against a far wall, the back of my sweat-coated suit sticking to the hive blocks like Velcro.

It was at this particular juncture that I became aware of a rather frightening development-an *inner-system malfunction,* if you will. It seemed the use of actual words or vocal output of any kind, to include shrieks, screams, or even a garbled whine was no longer a viable option. A complete system shutdown wasn't far behind, as the effects of extreme shock had no doubt begun to take a rather massive toll on the old noggin circuitry. Translation: I was losing control at warp speed. Hallucination-induced alternate universe or not, I realized I had about two minutes to find a way out before such an option became utterly moot and the simple task of counting my fingers and toes was beyond all mental capacity.

Removing the baton from my belt, I slung it at a downward arc 'til the spear extended before taking a few ticks to re-pump the B&G back to

177

maximum blast level. Whatever the hell those things were, they weren't about to feed on Jack Wyatt Barton's carcass without a bloody mess of a brawl to be had beforehand. I'd already decided to save the grenades until the very last, possibly not initiating denotation 'til I was down to my last breath. Definitely a scenario befitting the old 'blaze of glory' send-off if there'd ever been one.

The pod closest to me, four or five steps to my left give or take, ripped open like it'd been hacksawed from the inside, dousing me in a white fluid that reeked of ammonia. So there I stood, soaked in larvae afterbirth, not to mention a small amount of my own urine, as the bulky contents fell to the ground with a low, muffled crunching noise. I swear it sounded like a bull elephant taking a dump atop a pile of dried leaves, or at least as I would envision such a weird racket.

In attempting to wipe the milkfish fluid from my mask, I only managed to smear it until any and all visuals were lost for at least a minute or so. In the meantime, I heard similar births transpire all around, each footstep I took sloshing as if I were treading ankle-high swamp water. Note of later importance: I'd soon discover my flashlight had joined a growing list of P. O. W items, human and otherwise.

Eventually ripping the mask free in sheer frustration, I slung the damn thing into parks unknown, figuring I now had much bigger concerns than post- pesticide aftereffects. Meantime, the 'disco' lighting had grown more frantic if anything; a spastic hit or miss visual proposition wherein each and every movement was akin to those gradual, stop-motion movie effects. Turned out to be a blessing, really, 'cause just as I managed to regain my bearings it became apparent that it was better *not* to see what I was sharing the room with.

Half-stepping to the center of the room, at least until the tips of my boots connected with the outer perimeter of 'bone-hill', I watched 'em circle me like cultists prepping a virgin sacrifice. Buck naked and covered in purplish goop that resembled melted crayons, the process of identification was elementary despite the matted hair and overabundance of bared flesh. To my immediate left stood Virgil Hobbs, slack-jawed and shoulders slumped, his mouth hanging open like a kitchen drawer. Delbert Prescott stood to his right, his prominent gut pouching out and down like a soggy donut, his slug-like lower lip stooped just low enough to reveal a set of blackish teeth that resembled Tick-Tacks dipped in tar.

Next came the less-than-dynamic duo of James Bohannon and Gil Braggs, the formers freakishly large manhood standing semi-erect, a fact even he seemed completely oblivious to. The good doctor possessed a similarly bland expression, a constant stream of after-birth trailing from both nostrils like faucets in dire need of a new washer.

Last but not least, fronting me from less than three feet away, stood Gaven McCloud, his usual boyish grin replaced by a frozen sneer that brought to mind old World War II POW photos I'd seen as a child displaying the ultimate in human misery and suffering.

Despite the obvious, that being their present state of nudity and/or mindlessness, all five shared one additional trait-their eyes were glowing, red-hot embers void either whiteness or pupils. Talk about the ultimate creep-out scene-I'm talking straight out of 'Body Snatchers', man.

"He-hey…um, guys…c-can you…can you hear…can you… understand me?"All of the sudden, despite the stark fear gripping every fiber of my being, I couldn't help but guffaw at my own behavior-enunciating every syllable like a lost tourist who figures speaking English very, *very* slowly equates to everyone understanding what he's babbling about. All the time I'd been gripping the B&G wand in a vice, even managing to bend it somewhat. It wasn't until Delbert Prescott took a wobbly step forward, his mouth stretching wide as to yawn, that I instinctively aimed the nozzle his way. Poor guy's red-shaded eyes were bugging like coffee saucers, his forehead and jaws inundated with bulging veins. It was like he was straining to take a dump the size of your basic SUV.

"What…what's wrong, Delbert? Are you…you don't look too…you…feel okay, man? Del-…" I somehow refrained from spraying until the gentle Brit's entire head split apart like a honeydew melon from an axe blade, sending yet another tidal wave of purplish fluid my way. I managed to side-step the majority of the deluge and watched the headless form of Delbert Prescott slump to the floor to my immediate left. A single tick later, Virgil Hobbs' bloated coconut performed a similar implosion to my right. Falling to one knee, I thought I caught of

180

glimpse of our former 'team leader's' dislodged nose float by in a sea of purplish-black.

Executing what I'm sure was a rather pathetic combat-roll which concluded with a vicious rattling of teeth and badly battered ribs once a far wall ended my momentum, I posed on one knee while firing the B&G at full blast. Can't really say to whom or what I'd been aiming at, as by that time the rest of the team had joined in on the self-implosion fad, all that is, save one.

Gaven McCloud stumbled forward, stepping over the other's headless carcasses, his hands held out in true 'sleepwalking zombie' fashion.

"Where's Beth, Cloudy? Have you…seen Beth, man?" I heard myself ask as he grew to within a mere two to three feet where I stood, basically having boxed myself in like cornered prey. I have to admit to being a bit self-proud at my concern for someone's safety beside my own at that point-says a lot about the relationship Beth and I had established through the years. The two of us hadn't shared a bed in eons, but a similar closeness still existed. I would hope she felt the same.

"What the hell's going on, Cloudy? What…what did you guys… *find* down here, man?"

Stopping less than an arm's length away, McCloud then raised both arms as if he were surrendering, those maroon-shaded eyes rolling back in his head to reveal a slight layer of whiteness that stood out like twin lighthouse beacons in comparison.

"Answer me, Gaven. . . WHY WASN'T I WARNED?" I screamed, undoubtedly more out of fear than frustration,"*WHAT THE FUCK DID YOU PEOPLE GET INTO DOWN HERE?*" But no answer was forthcoming…not that I'd really expected one.

Hysterics will almost always overwhelm good sense. These weren't the same people I'd met and trained with the previous two days. Fact was, it was a safe bet they weren't *people* at all. Pale facsimiles at best, I'd wager. No hard evidence to back that up, of course, but what transpired in the next two minutes seemed to back it up the opinion, 'cause nothing remotely human can possibly mutate so rapidly. No way, Jose. Maybe we were talking clones, perhaps involving some sort of elaborate alien-abduction scenario. For the moment, it was damn near impossible to clearly speculate on such matters, much less pinpoint a solid, logical explanation.

His arms raised high in full 'touchdown' pose, Gaven McCloud's midsection began to swell and bloat 'til it was the size of a ten-gallon bladder before moving to his chest and throat. I swear the poor shit resembled something out of a H. G. Wells nightmare; half-man, half-bullfrog. That is, until the reason for the unnatural bulge spewed out of his mouth in a wave of black soot, basically pinning my hide to the wall in the process. Falling face-first into the quagmire, I began pulling handfuls from my face, head and neck. I felt their masses crunch and pop beneath my grip, not to mention what felt like a dozen stings and/or bites penetrate my gloves and so-called 'impenetrable' chem suit. Floundering about like a blind bull in a China shop, I wasn't able to ID their origin 'til I'd cleared my eyes somewhat. Now…I'd seen my share of Jagged-legged Centipedes, though usually in groups of ten or less. It's a damn site more intimidating looking down and seeing one's entire body bathed in the little green and yellow bastards, their snake-like torsos wriggling about like feeding maggots as razor-sharp leg blades slashed and carved.

It took at least a minute or so of frantic slapping, grabbing and tossing to rid my chest, groin and legs of the army that the McCloud-Thing had projectile vomited my way. In terms of coordination and reflexes, the previous half-hour had taken their toll, big time. I was one battered, beat-up pup, both from a physical and brain-box standpoint. By the time I *was* able to focus elsewhere, retrieving my B&G and Ultra- Spear after a short belly crawl, the entire room was in the midst if a mass transformed-and in far less than a *positive* manner.

All the fallen corpses had collapsed face-up, though that specific fact was damned hard to fathom at first since none possessed actual faces to speak of.

Posed belly-up, each was hatching a particular insect from wide chasms located at their chest, belly, or the hole that had been the home to their individual facial features. I think I recall cursing in tongue at this point, scrambling to my feet while frantically pumping the B&G for at least the third time in a half-hour. As it was, I found myself hapless to the ancient 'train wreck' theory, thus frozen securely in place and unable to pull my tearing eyes from the horrors on display.

Amazingly, I was able to ID each rampaging species individually. This brought to light yet another ancient cliché proven true yet again: one can never quite separate themselves from their chosen field, no matter how dire the circumstances. For yours truly, it was simply force of habit-sounds lame but it's the lone explanation I can give for why I stood there like a damn fool ogling as long as I did.

Thus, the hall of horrors sprang forth the following abominations, though not in any particular order since my frazzled memory banks are beyond performing such miracles:

The *Gaven McCloud/Host*: I watched a brigade of centipedes cart the man's severed, horrifically mutilated head to a far corner of the room as if attempting a daring robbery from the remainder of the herd. Meantime, his pale, lifeless torso was systemically stripped to the bone from the inside/out, several detached limbs hoisted away like floating cordwood.

The *Delbert Prescott/Host:* Mounds of Skin-Bore ants poured from the chest and abdominal cavity, tearing away strips of flesh, tissue and sinew in the process.

The *Gil 'Doc Death' Braggs/Host*: From the facial chasm and fist-sized hole in the neck region skittered hundreds if not thousands of Bloated-Belly Scorpions, some of the Green-Streak and still others of the Brown-Streak variety. As with the Skin-Bore Ants, the escaping hoards were equally merciless

184

upon exiting. They ripped away at the hosts' shell, using those ever-lethal, wildly slashing tails and vice-like claws to reduce the good doctor to a skeletal mishmash in their trampling wake.

The *James Bohannon/Host*: Never one to be outdone, Mister Muscles spewed forth a lethal combo of both Black Recluse and Fiddler Widow Spiders, the latter of which quickly busied themselves by spinning their flesh-dissolving web about the host's oversized biceps, shoulders and pectoral regions. Rarely a species to sit idly by, the deadly Recluse clan pitched in with a multitude of tissue-decomposing bites that soon turned the self-proclaimed 'Ebony Assassin's' normally Roman Temple-like physique into a pile of quivering black bile.

The *Virgil Hobbs/Host*: Our team leader and former Exterminator of The Year in the great state of Pennsylvania suffered perhaps the grisliest demise of all; first birthing a mountain of carnivorous Jamaican Red-Stripe Roaches from a basketball-sized hole in his gut and subsequently being devoured by same.

Even in my dazed, numbed state, I must've figured it was only inevitable that those enjoying the feast turn in my direction, and I'll be damned if I was just gonna stand around and become just another lunch item specialty from the 'Exterminator' section of the menu. Sad to say, but for the first time since strolling into that haunted hive, I put all thoughts of Beth's well-being aside and decided that saving my *own* ass was priority one.

I hadn't taken more than three steps to my left, hoping to relocate the 'in' door, when everything began to change...and I'm not talking minute shit either...but big time, major alternations. One might say it appeared the second course in the massive bug buffet was being served, though the entrée in question came as a hell of a shock.

I watched the walls open up all around me as the hive ports, each of which were sized approximately six by eight inches, popped open like soda cans before spewing forth their bloated contents onto the feeding masses within. Sincerely, it was like watching the Super-Bowl of all 'bug-outs'. Ban pun aside, I'd have given my Kingdom, or at least the contents of a rather pathetic savings account, for a suitable escape route...

BUG OUT, PART ELEVEN

Peephole into the Abyss

In the surreal aftermath of witnessing my Pest Control peers and former icons of the business ravaged like rotted corpses beneath Maggot Mountain, I found it remarkably easy to shrug off the entire hellish scene as nothing more than an elaborate hoax. Honestly, what could've possibly transpired in a ten to twelve minute span to turn 'em all into walking parasite hosts? I had to convince myself, in lieu of really having no logical choice, that Gaven, Delbert and the rest were indeed still alive and like me, fighting like mad to both stay alive and maintain a semblance of sanity. Self-preservation, baby, both mind and body.

That's what it's all about in this life, after all.

All that said, scaling a living wall as hive ports imploded and filled the room with the self-same hybrid Assassin Bugs we'd discovered in the stairwells was a damn site harder to swallow, as was the insect massacre that ensued upon the arrival of their several-million-bug army. Have to say those bloated bad boys were anything but picky, gorging on any and *everything* that moved. Never thought I'd see the day when healthy populations of Fiddler Widows, Jamaican Flesh rippers or Bloated-Belly Scorps would willfully flee from any scrap, but there it was reflected in my badly bloodshot peepers. Hell's Bell's if even the Skin-Bores weren't trying to high-tail it to safer climes. To no avail on all counts, by the way. Regardless of sex, race, religion, species or subspecies, each was treated with equal viciousness by the new bully on the predatory block. Black Recluses and Widows alike were cut to shreds and subsequently devoured: Jagged Centipedes were segmented or swallowed whole, as were the dreaded spear-tailed Scorpions, whose usually deadly sting seemed to have little or no effect on the hybrid Assassins, who shrugged off every counter attack with a psychotic, insatiable determination to first sadistically murder before gorging on their insect brethren. Don't get me wrong; I wasn't feeling pity for the nasty little bastards.

Strongly to the contrary, I'm of the belief each got what they so richly deserved, given their individual legacies. Besides, I was waaaayyy too busy trying to stay unnoticed while tip-toeing around the madness searching for an exit.

Funny, but I hadn't taken conscious notice of the crunch 'n munch concerto filling both ears…that is, 'til the lights went out-a rather grave occurrence that forced me to instantly take note. Guess it's the old 'lose one sense and the others gain added sensitivity' syndrome. Whatever the reason, suddenly it sounded as if I'd fallen into a dump-truck loaded with corn flakes and a busload of starving bulimic's. The hell with an escape route. . . the Kingdom keys would've gladly been handed over to the first animal, veggie, or mineral possessing a working flashlight, candle, or book of dry matches.

As bad as the total darkness was, and bad it most assuredly was, it barely rated compared to the creepy-crawly sensation all about my feet, legs and groin. Damn things were coating my suit like syrup on hotcakes, and it was surely only a matter of time before their helter-skelter road-map led to my unguarded facial region. With that in mind, I took off in a wild, blind sprint, not really giving a good shit about a final destination.

I felt the ground collapse beneath my feet about the same time the majority of the feeding frenzy racket went mute. Though I do faintly recall a hapless 'weightless' feeling, the subsequent landing was a complete mystery. Probably a good thing, that.

Seems I had fallen into a tunnel similar to the one I'd entered when searching for Beth, though there were a few subtle changes. While circular in shape and coated in a thick film of the same glutinous goop, this particular pathway was easily twice as large in circumference, its concave ceiling a good twelve to fifteen feet high. Foreboding as it sounded, I couldn't help but wonder just what might require such a roomy passageway. Being as I'd managed to toss away or misplace every weapon in the arsenal save the Ultra-Spear, all sense of self-defense related security was as hopelessly lost as yours truly.

"C'mon now, Jack-O, how's about looking on the bright side for once?

Maybe it's an exit to the surface. Yeah, that's it. Leads straight up to main street New Horizons. . ." I murmured; beaten, battered, out of breath and nearing as complete a physical and mental meltdown as I'd ever experienced. Again I dwelled: where the hell was everybody?

"Yeah, my big old hairy white ass it does. More than likely the passageway straight to hell."

As if to punctuate such optimism, I heard a wet plopping sound and turned to see a colossal pile of bloated Assassin's falling through the same hole I'd hoped would be my salvation from their feeding masses.

Really should've known better...Lady Luck had apparently flown the coop for the duration, and I couldn't blame the cowardly bitch a single iota. Lord knows if the option had been available, I'd have done the very same. As it was, I continued to pick 'em up and put 'em down as fast as humanly possible, though the old internal engine was pretty near blowing flumes by then, adrenaline be damned. Dangerous ebbing energy level aside, I was determined that death by predatory bug wasn't the way this boy was going out. Was this attitude dictated by something as foolish as professional pride? Perhaps, but the idea of dying at the hands, or in this case claws and/or pinchers of a species you'd been paid to eradicate for over a decade just seemed.... wrong in so many varied fucking ways. Seemed like the ultimate Science-Fiction cliché: unabashed 'predator becomes the prey' tripe.

Thirty or forty yards further down the tunnel and the foul-smelling swamp glop was ankle deep. I didn't bother, or should I say *dare*, turn around to see if the little shits were gaining on me. The increased volume of the 'million-bug' march's incessant whine, plus the sinking feeling the point-men would soon be crawling up my calf was all the proof I needed.

A sharp right-hand curve approached just as I stood knee-deep in the quagmire. Splashing my arms like a panicky swimmer going under for the third time, I even managed to swallow a batch and couldn't help but be reminded of the only time I ever willfully ingested oysters. Worse yet, this particular mouthful of slime not only stunk like recently evacuated diarrhea, but held the taste and texture of rotten egg-yolks.

Another ten to twelve yards and the sewer water grew mercifully shallower, and I double-timed it through the curve and straight into another fucking dead end. Whipping out my trusty Ultra-Spear, I began to frantically slash and bat the hive ports, hoping for the same imploding effect as the last. Meanwhile, the combination scuttling/humming noises grew near, though the thunderous pounding at my temples did manage to drown them out somewhat. As the spear seemed to be having little effect on the wall, I could practically feel my very life-source begin to slip away like a clock with rapidly weakening batteries. Damned weird, but I was probably less than a full minute from being insect-filler, and my mind was suddenly, inexplicably filled with thoughts of Beth. It was damned obvious, or perhaps tragic is a better word, that I had never truly realized the level of admiration I had for that woman.

The charging, rampaging, ravenous horde grew ever closer just as my inner gas tank hit the dreaded 'E' mark and I collapsed to my knees with my back pinned against the very blockade that would spell the end of my days. I thought of my deceased parents, my younger sister raising a fine family in the beauteous mountains of Vale, and of course…I thought again of Beth. I thought of her smell, her radiant smile and biting humor-those Mister Spock eyebrows she so meticulously cultivated and cocked at timed intervals-those perfectly rounded buttocks and perky tits. Impossibly, I swear I even felt the beginning twinges of an erection. Lord, I guess in the end it really *does* come down to sex. Buttered sentimentality be damned, it all comes down to bumping uglies.

Leaning my head back, I closed my eyes, sucked in a deep, labored breath and awaited the inevitable. Apparently, a foregone conclusion that was never fated to be. Guess it wasn't quite 'my time', after all.

Don't really know what to compare the sensation too, except perhaps being sucked into the engine of a seven-oh-seven. The initial jolt must've rendered me unconscious, though in-between naps I do recall dribs and drabs of the journey itself. Once pulled through the wall, I was then dragged at what seemed like an astonishing speed, again-hard to tell while drifting in and out of La-La Land-through a narrow tunnel that seemed just large enough to accommodate my bulk. Along the way I felt my suit strip away, along with what I hoped was a minimal amount of flesh. As such, I dreamed of rebirth, of replenishment, of new beginnings. Hey, beats the hell out of the alternatives.

Like the majority of the trek itself, the conclusive landing that followed was equally enigmatic. I awoke with a thundering headache, blurred vision and perhaps a cracked rib or two. Standing on creaky knees, my nostrils flared to a stout scent that might've been either raw sewage or perforated gut, or perhaps a sickening combination of both. Where I'd landed, it appeared to be nothing more than a larger variation of the room before it…a circular, tunnel-like chasm whose walls were similarly infested with hive ports and the like. I wouldn't notice the vein-like, blackish cords dominating the ceiling portion until it was far too late to investigate or even speculate on their origin.

Slinging the wetness from my hands, I rubbed both eyes as to clear away the cobwebs. Stumbling blindly, I felt something solid brush against my left shoulder and figured I'd found the nearest wall, though the object did seem to give way from my intrusion.

Once the baby blues refocused to the sixty to seventy percent range, I was able to ID the object as it swayed like a pendulum blade a mere two feet from where I stood open-mouthed.

"B-Beth? Je-Jesus…Beth…"

She hung half-in, half-out of a surprisingly small, ivory-colored larvae pouch, her head leaning hard to the left as if she'd suffered some serious neck and/or back trauma.

Her formerly spiked hair was matted to her skull in rounded clumps that held yellow and crimson streaks in equal abundance.

"Beth, are you…can you hear me? It's J-Jack, babe…Jack-O…" Her left eye popped open just as I leaned in and I yelped like a scared grade-schooler stabbed in the ass-cheeks by a sewing needle.

"J-J-Ja-ccck?" she stuttered weakly, purplish spittle dribbling onto her chin and bubbling at the corners of her trembling lips.

"Yeah…yeah, babe…Jack-O's right here. Are…are you…al-alright?"

"Do…do I…l-look aw-alright, dumb-a-ass?"

I couldn't refrain from laughing aloud, despite the obvious direness of the situation. A smart-ass, hard-as-nails chick to the very end, my dear Bethy.

"What happened, Beth? I…I lost you past the power grid and…couldn't find you again."

While speaking, I reached over and took her left hand into my own. Hers was ice-cold and stiff…lifeless-a dead man's appendage.

"Did…did you…s-see th-the others…J-Jack? Did…you see what…what they…"

She was cut off by a series of violent, hacking coughs, the last of which brought forth a veritable geyser of maroon that splattered my throat and bare chest.

"Uh…uh, yeah. I…I did see 'em, as a matter of fact. Not…to long ago. I…saw them all."

Her right eye, which was brow-less and matted shut as if nailed into place, wriggled and strained until it too opened with a gruesome ripping sound. It was several ticks before I noticed that a small portion of the lid had torn away and had settled onto her jaw-line like a stray leaflet. It wasn't long after that it became hideously apparent why the cocoon was so damn compact, as jagged thigh bone protruded from its bottom portion like broken tent stakes and thick red droplets fell from the frazzled edges.

"Then...you...you...saw   what...they had...become?"

"Be-become?" I asked wearily, actually finding myself backing away a step, unable not to speculate on what horrors had befallen her while I'd stumbled about like a damn fool for who knows how long. First and foremost, why had only her lower legs been eaten away? Believe it not, in all that I'd seen and experienced since entering the darkest lairs of that fucking pit, I was still very capable of delivering an involuntary shiver at the mere thought.

"Wha-what they had...me-the-mathe-...meta-mor-pho-sized into..."

"Uh, yeah...you...you could say that...I...I guess."

"Te-tell me....J-Ja-ccck, w-were th-...were they...be-beautiful?"

Lord help me, I almost wept at not only the question and its dreamy, melancholy delivery, but in the fact that despite her present state of extreme delirium and physical mutilation, Beth Cambridge still managed to appear downright radiant. With what little motivation remained in my tattered soul, I took a deep breath and proceeded to lie through my teeth as a favor to probably the best friend I ever had.

"They...were really...something to see, Beth. It was...well, what you said...beautiful."

195

"J-J-Jack…oh…will I…be beau…beautiful. . . too? Tell me…tell me I will…J-Jock…J-Jack. Tell me…I-I-I'll be…beau…like them."

With no hesitation, I stepped forward and gently placed a hand against the side of her face, which boiled with fever.

"Oh, you will, Bethy. You'll be…the most beautiful of all." Once again, her right eye-lid lifted, but this time only partially."Just…just like a…b-b-butter…butterfly, ri-right, Ja-Jack?"

In replying, my voice hitched just a tad.

"Damn right, Beth. The most glorious butterfly man's ever laid his eyes on. Breath-taking…exquisite…a one in a million beauty."

"Y-you…you're…f-full of s-s-shit, b-boss. Th-that's w-why…I…l-l- love…ya…"

With that, my best friend and former lover sighed deeply and expired with my hands cradling both sides of her head. As hard as it was, I was grateful for her expedient passing in my presence, as watching her suffer so had already begun to hatch thoughts of a possible mercy killing-something I'm pretty damn sure I could've never gone through with.

"Boss-man…loves you too, Bethy. Boss-man…always did. Boss-man wishes…he could've…saved you…but he can't even…I really don't think he can even…save himself."

Not sure how long I stood and watched Beth's lifeless body, or what remained of it, sway slowly to and fro like a tire-swing from a thick oak branch. Might've been as short a duration as a few minutes or as lengthy as ten-plus. In eventually backtracking several steps, I looked down upon my own nakedness and pondered my old friend's talk of transformation and metamorphosis.

Perhaps this was the beginning of my own, I pondered aloud, my voice deep with hoarseness.

"Butterfly? Nah, not this boy. *Vulture beetle*, maybe…perhaps even a *Black-Plague Mosquito*…but an ordinary member of the Moth family? Not a chance, baby…"

I recall shooting Beth a final glance as in final salute when the floor, walls and ceiling began to shake and rumble as if guided by a nearby volcanic eruption.

"Awwww, what the hell *now*?"

Falling backward, I managed to lean onto my right elbow and steady myself just enough to become a fascinated observer to this latest potential catastrophe. Sounds nuts, I concede, but the whole blasted shooting match was beginning to have it comical aspects. I mean, for *shits sake*, how much mystery, suspense, and imminent danger can one man be expected to take without blowing a vital gasket, brain-matter wise?

Without a hint of fear, no doubt an emotion that had long since gone dormant since Beth's passing, I watched the tunnel ground and walls swell and bloat all around me, like some warped funhouse attraction ala the old standby 'house of mirrors'. Hundreds (thousands?) of hive ports plopped free from their assigned slots like scorched popcorn kernels, while the tunnel as a whole seemed on the verge of collapsing inward on itself. Glancing up, I noted a series of thick, cord-like ropes running along the

197

ceiling like tree roots. As the commotion grew ever stronger and my legs and lower torso was being tugged at by a mysterious suction, I noticed the cords pulsating like…dare I speculate…like coursing veins. One of the roots/cords sustained a serious gash just as I was being pulled forward by the stout, unrelenting pull originating from a westerly direction, spewing forth a fine, tar-shaded mist that brought to mind spillage from a punctured oil line.

Slung about like a pine straw in a monsoon, I bounded from floor to wall to ceiling, positioning both hands in front of my face as to at least ward off the majority of possible head traumas. Predictably, I lost consciousness several times along the way. There was little doubt I'd suffered a concussion, though the severity of which remained to be seen, and my ribs throbbed and ached with every thump, thud or even glancing blow.

As fate would have it, it was in fact those self-same bruised or possibly shattered inner appendages that awoke me to the cold hard truth about my ordeal once the latest trek had momentarily been paused. Talk about your cramped confines, I felt like the proverbial milkshake sucked through a plastic straw-my arms were pinned forcefully at my sides while my knees were shoved together like twin fractures within the same plaster cast.

For whatever reason, call it fate…kismet…destiny…the fleshy tube I found myself jammed into had a tiny rip just above my left shoulder-a built-in peephole just large enough for me to utilize once I'd craned my neck downward a bit.

Its truly hard to describe-damned near impossible actually-the feelings that emerged as a result of my half-minute to forty-five second 'sneak preview'…but if I were forced to sum them up in a handful of words, I guess 'royally duped' or 'played for the ultimate fool' might suffice. I mean, it was all right there in front of me the whole time…so many clues…so many obvious hints. As is one of the primary weaknesses of man, I'd been hijacked by a woeful lack of imagination- my own sense of wonder and awe rendered impotent by the inbred theory that mankind as a society has no worthy peer.

To the contrary, I saw proof…up close and far too personal that the aforementioned theory is sprinkled in no small amount of steaming horse manure, or should I say…and far more appropriately…steaming *bug excrement*? She was a true wonder…this *Queen*-not merely a colossal goddess of immense physical magnitude, but a biological and scientific marvel that even the most jaded entomologist might well define as *the* textbook case of nature-gone- fucking-amok, emphasis on the 'F' word. As for your atypical layman's description, *'that's one big, ugly som' bitch'* would cover it quite nicely, and not without a substantial layer of truth at that. I could only estimate her size at roughly that of a parked seven-four-seven, and with a pincher span of at least fifty feet on either side, though this was hard to determine since the four separate slice 'n dicers were bent at the center as to prop up the massive torso.

"Well, hellllllooooo, big mama," I managed to whimper, my entire body coated in chill-bumps.

She sat atop a scaly, hot-air balloon-sized birthing sac that was partially translucent, thus allowing at least a working glance at the multitude of as-of-yet- un-hatched inhumanity packed within. There was no way to even semi- accurately predict the number of infantile mantis-hybrids stuffed inside that pulsating bug-uterus, though from where I lay a few million might well have been an underestimation. Just as mind-boggling, if not more so, where the dozens of larvae pods hanging about, most of which appeared to hold similar human remains as what I'd witnessed with Beth, while I spotted several with canine features and at least one that appeared to be the front end of a horse. A few of the humans, at least the ones still possessing heads and/or faces, were easily identified as being African-American,, while the one Hispanic representative was still wearing a bright-yellow hard-hat atop his head. It wasn't a difficult assumption to figure the former were past tenants of the recently demolished projects, with the latter being one of the missing construction workers who aided in said demolition.

Regardless, it was a given that the starved little shits weren't the least bit picky in terms of potential menu items, especially when shooting straight from the birthing pouch and up to the dinner table. Ah, how sweat the treat, no *matter* the meat. I could only guess the feeders we'd run across in the stairwell had merely been defectors from the kingdom. The chasm which held her was a smoke-filled, dimly lit cavern roomy enough to house a luxury liner, yellowish flames periodically shooting from the few cracks I was able to distinguish in its stony housing.

There was yet other anomaly I'd noticed just as the suction grew stronger at my feet and legs and I was so rudely whisked away from my own little 'spy tunnel'. A series of intestine-like appendages, almost like feeding tubes of some type, snaked out from a separate portion of the Queen's gigantic underbelly. All were tinted a dark brown and not the least bit transparent, unlike the birthing sac. Weirdest thing was, all of 'em punctured the surrounding rock walls and ceiling surrounding the Queen, looking every bit like heater or AC ducts sewn from living flesh. I'd only begun to ponder their use within the grand scheme when the 'pea sucked through a straw' effect came back into play and the mysterious journey continued.

Chalk it up to the lunacy of the moment, but I could've sworn the Queen's massive, wondering left orb, the one that had been stationed in the same direction as my temporary peep-hole, shifted a bit and stared directly at me just as I was pulled away. Again, probably just a trick of both mind and bloodshot eye...

BUG OUT, PART TWELVE

Chemical Overload

The detonator, though remarkably light, felt leaden and slick in my palm, like an oiled TV remote forged from granite. Perhaps it was just a matter of my own physical weakness...nothing a fresh shot of inner-adrenalin couldn't fix.

With both my ticker and pulse rate zooming along at turbo speed, I was getting sharper by the beat. At first I had a hard time believing, much less accepting, the lucky hand I'd been dealt, especially considering the woeful lack of same that had dogged us all from step one of that damnable journey. Just a matter of being due, I'd wager-*overly* due at that. Still, everything that could go right in terms of possible survival had done just that, pieces falling perfectly into place like a fixed jigsaw puzzle constructed by magnetic means. Just to place things in their proper place, chronological wise, said lucky streak had begun thusly:

Lucky SOB Incident Number One:

Spit out like bagged trash from a piped chute, I managed to overshoot the larvae sac destined to become my home; the equivalent of a tortilla wrap to those starving mantis infants. Miraculously, probably a one-in-a-thousand shot at best, my left foot had bent just enough to the outside to catch the outer edge of the opened sac, knocking me off-balance and flipping me head-over-heels onto the gore-soaked flooring instead. I peered up to watch the sac jiggle around like a boxer's speed-bag. Repulsive, one might ask? Damn straight, though paling sadly in comparison to the realization that the body-tunnel that had sucked me into the pit was more than likely an extension of Big Mama's internal organs-i. e…a bug intestine, if you will. In a word…*yeeech*. As for my less-than-graceful landing, my left hand and right foot had quite possibly joined my ribs as hair-line fracture victims. Ignoring this latest series of maladies, I quickly bounced up onto my knees-greatly appreciating the fact I wasn't rolled up and packaged like a stuffed bean burrito.

Lucky SOB Incident Number Two:

In her constant state of continuous motherhood and the numerous duties contained therein, 'Big Mama' Queen herself had yet to turn and notice the food packaging discrepancy. It certainly didn't hurt that my assigned sac was stationed to her rear on the western end of the cavern, meaning she would've had to perform a one-eighty in order to spot my crouching nakedness. Wasn't real sure she even possessed such flexibility while perched atop the birthing sac, but it was only a matter of time before one of her assigned *sentinels* spotted me and announced it to the rest of the clan. Roughly the size of pit-bull pups, they were stationed near and around her combination partitions/pinchers, two to three deep at each claw. Like rotating security beacons, each would execute a complete turnabout every thirty seconds or so, no doubt to ensure the birth and feeding session checklists were being followed to a tee. As it was, the relative darkness, much of which was provided by the queen's own bulk, provided me a full minute or more to search out a suitable stalagmite formation.

Lucky SOB Incident Number Three:

I spotted the weaponry a relatively short rock toss away, no more than twenty or so feet from the V-shaped rock-mass I'd ducked behind. There were two B&G turbo rifles with packs and several Intruder Grenades strewn about, not to mention the Holy Grail of extermination it's own beauteous self, that being the one-and-only MaxForce Flusher unit. I had to assume Virgil and the other teams had at least made it this far, only to be cut down and subsequently forced into the native's 'boiling pot', so to speak. Pushing such grisly thoughts aside, if it had been at all possible to do so, I could've sprouted the Mount Kilimanjaro of erections at that very moment. Despite the temporary rush of elation, two potential obstacles still loomed heavy. *One*: how to get to the weapons stash without being spotted. *Two*: Were all or *any* still in working condition? With no time to waste, I'd surely find an answer soon enough.

Lucky SOB Incident Number Four:

In backtracking a bit concerning the MaxForce Flusher, I'd noticed two of the five spray nozzles were stationed just to the right of the queen's birth sac with the remaining three scattered about the cavern in ten to twenty yard intervals.

Talk about your perfect positioning, it was a chance-however slim-to cut off a portion of the snake's head, or at least cripple the ugly bitch a smidgen. This again depending on not only the equipment's workability, but my own talent in figuring out how to initiate the detonator before becoming bug-chum. As it stood, I figured I'd have fifteen to thirty seconds max on that little item. Then again, I'd always considered myself a fast learner. With that in mind, no sterner test would I ever face.

Sucking in several strained, smoke-infested breaths that did little but cause my throbbing ribs to bark ever louder, I made a mad dash towards the discarded weaponry, the cavern's wet, slick surface allowing me to slide and glide to a relatively smooth stop. It had mostly been a downhill jog to the weapons site, and I could only hope the sudden drop-off and dramatic concave shape of the grounds would keep me out of bug's-eye view. Still, I did my damnedest to keep the noise level to a minimum while loading up for battle, going so far as to hold in what I feared might be a rather loud, echoing fart.

Nope, this boy wasn't gonna be a mutated swarm's latest meal due to not being able to control passing gas. All that said, I'd have once again gladly given up the keys to the mythical Kingdom for a single dose of Bean-O.

I scooped up the B&G Turbo first, slinging the connecting backpack across my bare back and pumping her double-barreled cylinder to maximum output level before kneeling to snag two of the intruder grenades, placing them in one of the pack's two available side-pockets.

All the while, I kept a wandering eye peeled on Big Mama's hired sentries, none of which had apparently spotted me during the sprint.

Side-stepping over in a low-crouch, I cupped the MaxForce unit's palm- sized remote and gave its outer workings a quick once-over. Since no one except Virgil had received any actual 'OJT' on the device, I feared it might take some figuring out. Being that time was definitely a valued commodity, I was damned relieved to discover its directions for use a matter of simplicity in itself. Basically an 'amount' setting in regards to how much pesticide to use, followed by a sequence of tiny yellow buttons allowing separate nozzle usage, and finally the 'initiate' and 'abort' buttons, both conspicuously shaded in dark red. The *Prep Treatment* feature could be set in timed increments starting at one minute up to a full hour. As for aborting said mission, one had all the way until the five second mark to shut down.

Couldn't help but grin. In retrospect, I should've known it wasn't exactly gonna be Calculus. After all, we are talking *exterminators,* for Christ's sake.

Using the wet clay/dried blood caked forefinger of my right hand, I quickly set the amount used as 'ALL-Full Flush'-ditto for the five available nozzles-then set the Prep Treatment feature for exactly two minutes. Talk about fishing in the dark,

I had no earthly idea how long I'd need to first seek out and then utilize a possible escape route, making the abort feature a damned valuable one. Shoot the works too late, I'd be half-eaten flesh-pudding along with the bugs -fire 'em too soon and it'd be pretty much the same ugly scene, only minus as many bite- marks. Needless to say, I kept a thumb loosely parked atop that handy-dandy 'cut-off' button as 'Operation Exit Tunnel' began in earnest.

I hadn't scaled more than twenty yards of cavern wall before I heard the first sentry shriek out like a combination Yodel Cricket/Banshee Beetle.

Talk about kicking it into a gear you didn't know you even possessed, suddenly I was picking 'em up and putting 'em down like an Olympic sprinter, dodging the occasional stalagmite formation and trying like hell not to break my fool neck. My feet were already numb, bloody stumps from the tunnel-drag that had led me into the Queen's lair. I just added 'em to the growing list of cuts and fractures-hardly missing a beat in-between limps. For a split-second I thought, Beth would've been so proud to see the old man moving with such determination and purpose, regardless of the full-blown hysterical fear driving the performance.

Never daring to glance back, I nevertheless heard the insect chorus grow louder and more distinct at my back. Side-stepping a series of jagged stones and a rippling, black puddle of unknown origin, I turned a sharp right and spotted the tunnel opening thirty to forty feet ahead. Size-wise it was nothing to shout about-with its three to four feet circumference opening and darkened interior-I might well be diving head-first into a rabbit-hole that either narrowed to snake size somewhere down the line or dead-ended after a twenty-foot crawl. It wasn't like there was much in the way of options. I un-slung the turbo rifle from my left shoulder as I began hitting the brakes, figuring I had at least thirty more seconds before the MaxForce flooding ensued. Logically, the aforementioned thumb had now strategically slid a half-inch down, hovering just above the button reading 'initiate'. Might sound warped, but damned if I wasn't laughing like a Hyena on helium just as the whole blamed universe seemed to be going to shit. Upon whirling about and facing down my pursuers, said laughter rapidly transformed into an admittedly pathetic whine that came out sounding far too feminine. To the naked eye their numbers appeared as infinite as the assorted sizes packed within. Some, like the sentries, were freakishly large and lumbering, while still another representation were more kitten-sized and appeared quicker and more agile. Finally, there were the 'regulation' sized beasties, as tiny in stature as a run-of-the-mill assassin bug *slash* mantis, though blessed with lighting speed that assigned their larger numbers the 'point' position almost by proxy.

Aiming the B&G's single-sited barrel at the center of the charging hordes, my trigger finger contracted on instinct and a tad bit prematurely as the front row of potential targets were still eight or ten yards out of range.

Still, a veteran bug-stomper should never underestimate the importance of laying down an efficiently-placed perimeter spray, especially if the pest in question foolishly dashes directly into the hovering mist. I let off the trigger for a tick before resuming fire, slowly rotating the barrel as to increase the body count of those initially struck. I could hear a strained humming originate at the backpack and reverberating into the rifle's inner housing, no doubt the result of a constant spray delivered at the highest setting. Those bad-boys simply weren't constructed for such, and I prayed I didn't burn her out before draining the pack dry.

Have to confess, there was a second of stark fear as I watched the first row of mini-mantis' impact with the perimeter spray and dash through it seemingly unaffected. All such concerns were quickly dissipated, however, as they began to wriggle, spasm, and combat roll atop one another to escape the lethal vapors.

Even better, I felt my battered ticker soar when the lager versions did the same, some even lashing out at their own kind as the deadly 'contact –kill' poison sunk into their scaly hides, blurring both their vision and train of thought. I watched many whirl about and decapitate those closest to them with snapping pinchers, while others were simply stomped into segmented bug-puree by the lumbering, blinded masses.

Just as the spray pressure began to peter out, I saw that the big boys were now leading the charge, shoving aside their crippled and dead brethren without hesitation. The B&G was losing power fast, the spray-pressure roughly half its original strength. Tossing it aside after a final high-arced shot that caught one of the puppy-sized bastards dead-center in its wide-spread, grinding maw, I slung the pack to the ground and pulled out the intruder grenades.

Rearing back like a true fire-baller packing a ninety-plus mile an hour heater, I hurled that first one about knee-level high and watched it bounce forward like a skipped rock atop calm lake waters before igniting with a moist, spraying sound into a trio of hard-charging uglies. Their screams were ear- splitting in the cavern surroundings, like pained canine howls echoing inside a metal pipe. I'd already cocked back for a second toss, pump-faking as the front line charge quickly peeled away from their rapidly-melting comrades, then adjusted the throw to more of a high-arcing 'soft-toss'. Three or four more were splashed to oblivion upon its descent, though at least three dozen more survived and hardly missed a step as they made a frantic b-line my way.

Backing towards the tunnel entrance, I briefly turned my attention to the flush unit remote. Secure in the fact that my left forefinger was balanced atop the trigger button, I glanced back up for a final look-see.

The trampling hordes were less than fifteen yards away, resembling a maroon tidal wave headed straight for a beachhead named Jack Barton.

Looking past the ocean of scuttling insects, I saw the Queen had finally taken notice of all the commotion filling her birthing chamber. Twisting about on her bulbous throne, I heard the ripping, tearing sounds from beneath. Hard to fathom, but this giant behemoth-this biological marvel who was truly queen of all she surveyed, was actually threatened enough by one measly exterminator to physically abandon her sacred post. Flattered as I was, it was time to make like a leaf and blow, though not without making it an exit to remember. I pressed the execute button while airborne, leaping head-first into the tunnel as the queen's enraged shrieking filled the chamber like a dozen blaring Klaxon horns. All second-guessing aside, I could only hope the shit worked precisely as advertised.

Crawling up the pitch-black, slick-walled passage on my hands and knees, I found ironic humor in the fact that I no doubt resembled the very pest giving chase. There was the stinging disappointment of not being able to 'hang around' to witness the flusher unit in all its destructive glory as foamy gushers of the single strongest pesticide ever created shot into the air in stout steams, transforming all it came into contact with into instant bug-granules. I sure it would've been a royal kick in the pants to see the queen's armored shell riddled with acid-holes that eventually would find their way to a vital organ or two, or seeing those massive girders she called legs fracture and dissolve like overcooked linguine. On the negative side, even the slightest whiff of such lethal killing power would've left yours truly partially blind and gasping for breath.

As for my chosen path of escape, what had begun as a fairly snug, squared enclosure on a moistened plain, the terrain had gradually widened and headed uphill on a steep, dry grade that felt overtly familiar and that crunched beneath my weight, not unlike a dirt, gravel mix.

On the bright side, at least I was finally headed in the right direction, that being straight up. On the dark side, I couldn't see a damn thing and might well have been crawling straight into another of the queen's internal vacuum cleaners, only to end up bagged and served to her newest offspring like so much rolled sushi. Trying like hell to stay positive in the face of impending doom, I sped up the pace as much as my skinned, scarred, and battered appendages would allow, all the while inexplicably humming Henry Mancini's theme song to '*The Pink Panther*'. Beth would've howled in ecstasy at the prospects. With that, my heart ached like the worst tooth-ache imaginable. I was gonna survive, damn it, for her as much as myself. For her, and the rest of those recruited to die this day. Sentimental BS, some would say, about as sincere as a demon's promise. Well, fuck 'em, *I* say. Fuck 'em all, and the saddled Jackasses they rode in on.

To reiterate, stress equals profuse profanity in my own personal case, but at this juncture, I apologized to no one.

BUG OUT, PART THIRTEEN

A Mama's Rage

Did a shit-load of thinking on that half-hour-plus crawl, this for want of anything else to do save listening for the bug army possibly tailing me in the darkness. I thought back to the Hive Queen's lair and the flame-filled chasm near her birthing sac, and came to a conclusion straight from one of those old Sci-Fi pulp novels I used to read as a kid. Whatever these things were, be it insect or species unknown, I theorized they crawled from the earth's deepest pit via a recently developed crater. In his opening briefing, Pretty Boy Garrison had mentioned tremors causing foundation damages on the site and delaying construction…something about an unstable fault-line and that the local area had been long past due for a major quake.

Sounds nuts, but this would explain the fiery chasm, and more than likely the creatures themselves, their underground hive freed from forced imprisonment at the earth's core after Lord knows how many centuries. Those quakes didn't exactly awake a sleeping giant as much as provide a trail for 'em to blaze all the way to the surface.

I know, I know…maniacal rants from a recently crowned lunatic. But hey, it was as plausible a theory as anything I'd seen first-hand in the previous few hours.

The light was faint at first, barely a glimmer that appeared miles in the distance as my marathon crawl through the 'mole trail' continued unabated.

Dim brightened to pleasantly murky a few minutes later, and I thought my heart might well explode if not simply give out altogether. My escape route dead-ended as the light-source shone above through a squared hole in the hard clay ceiling.

Being that the old fear-meter had long since petered out, I didn't think twice before crawling through this newest entranceway. The passage, while only half as wide as the last, was blessed with a higher ceiling that allowed me to stand and walk forward while having to hunker down only a few inches, and while the aforementioned light was in reality less than the equivalent of a cheap Bic dangerously low on fluid, it sure beat the hell out of total darkness.

Within a few dozen feet, I spotted the edges of a badly rusted ladder leading to the light source and hopped aboard that bad-boy without hesitation, a possible collapse and subsequent fall be damned. Twenty-eight rungs later, *damn right* I counted, and I popped my head through the open space a two-by-two man-hole cover should've been occupying. The daylights full effect temporarily blinding me, I rolled onto the wet pavement and lay on my back, naked as a jaybird and rank as a skunk's asshole and not giving a good damn who might be offended by either condition. As a gentle rain slapped my face, I inhaled and exhaled greedily, as it felt like days since I'd filled the old internal air bags with *even* semi-fresh air. My eyes closed to the still-intrusive light, I was a nocturnal beast in the midst of re-transformation to normality, as at least what I had thought it to be.

I knew I had to rise-pull myself up, brush myself off and do a twenty-first century reenactment of Paul Revere's ride-to contact local authorities and warn them of the impending danger of what lay beneath the surface of New Horizon's pet project, but for several minutes I was at the mercy of a merciless exhaustion that was as relieving as it was crippling. If left alone in my weariness, there was little doubt I could lose a day or so via a long, leisurely ride on the Comatose Express. As it was, I was lucky to grab five full minutes of peace before being startled back into unreality by the sound of wailing sirens and screeching tires from a faraway distance. The cavalry to the rescue, perhaps? Yeah, *right*. With my track record to date, should've known better than to allow an optimistic thought to sneak in, no matter how minute. Pushing myself onto my knees with great difficulty, I cocked my head towards the source of all the commotion and deduced the origin to be near the interstate, about a mile and a half to the North of the New Horizons sub-division. Standing shakily, I took a quick inventory of the multiple gashes, scratches and cuts about my hands, arms and legs, most of which had already bled out and thus left a virtual roadmap of dried seepage behind. I shook off a brief dizzy spell and took off in a rambling jog directly down the center of what was listed on a nearby street sign as 'New Hope' road. Tempted as I was to spout such dramatic tripe as 'need some help here', 'somebody call nine-one-one' or even the criminally simplistic but normally effective 'help!', neither my tattered lungs or

215

severely parched throat was up to the task. Besides, it wasn't as if there were any residents to warn *slash* assist in a deserted, partially constructed sub-division.

As the rain's intensity noticeably increased and my flesh began to chill to uncomfortable levels, I took a hard right at 'New Revelations' road, just past a trio of brick town-homes still minus a fully erected wall, deck or section of roofing.

Hmmm…seems the brass at *New* Horizons didn't miss a trick in naming every street in the compound after themselves…subtle but just the least bit irritating, I found.

Braking at the intersection of 'New Revelations' and 'New Dawn' roads, I paused just long enough to catch a glimpse of one of the dark-blue 'Honor- Guard' security vans parked fifty yards or so to my left on Dawn. That's it! I exhumed with guarded excitement, there was at least a puncher's chance that one or more of the security guys had gotten out too, being that none had followed us inside the power grid level.

Predictably, all the good vibes drained away like weak radio reception once I reached the van, which was minus any passengers as well as locked up tight. In truth, I was hoping to find an empty uniform inside, if not a loaded weapon or two. It wasn't just my nakedness feeding the high degree of vulnerability, but a stout sense of dread that the dangers of below ground weren't far from scratching and clawing their way to the surface. Even in my frazzled condition, I wasn't yet dense enough to believe a single dumping of pesticide had

216

the potential to wipe out such an enormous army, twenty-plus gallons or not.

Similarly, there was the matter of that that semi-truck sized matriarch, the mental image of which initiated an instant break-out of fear-induced hives. To utilize the vernacular in the tradition of such luminaries as the late, great Gaven McCloud, *'that bug-bitch was a Triple-M threat: massive, menacing and mean.'*

The way I figured it, paranoia not withstanding, even if the majority of her ground troops had bit the big one in a tidal wave of Demon-X, Mama Egg-Hatch might well be looking for some serious payback in the aftermath of her own survival. It was a matter of parental pride, after all, not to mention a shot at some down and dirty retribution.

Following a brief sabbatical in which I actually considered breaking into the security van via a pass key shaped not so inconspicuously like a large, sharp-pointed rock, I instead followed New Dawn 'til it intersected with New Horizons Boulevard. Centering the freshly lain pavement, I crested a steep hill and spotted the admin building's east side less than twenty yards ahead. It looked weird from that particular angle, with its pentagon shape, flat roof and total lack of vegetation cover. The rain had eased up a tad by then, though puffy, motionless black clouds still hung low overhead as if to forewarn a new series of imminent downpours. Picking up the pace as much as I was able as a final surge or energy kicked in, I turned a corner at the buildings eastern edge as to enter through the front and almost instantly skidded to a stop, slipping onto one knee in the process and subsequently skinning that bad boy almost to the cap. I'm pretty sure I let fly with a flurry of obscenities in the aftermath, but more from what I was seeing than physical pain.

"Jesus...wept," I recall concluding, backing away into a relatively small dirt/gravel parking lot that was earmarked for 'MANAGERS ONLY' parking according to a wooden sign posted nearby.

Guess the old ticker still had some quality beats left in 'er, otherwise the mental checklist of horrors I was forced to endure would've caused a major work stoppage within the surrounding arteries. As if on cue to allow me a totally unobstructed view, the rain had stopped altogether.

Breaking down the approaching mob by rank and/or personal recognition, Floyd C. Garrison, AKA '*Pretty Boy Floyd*' was on point, followed by the good Professor, Ronald Godale, who lurched, stumbled and staggered just a step behind and two more to the left of his former boss. It would've been the ultimate understatement to say either man had seen better days, at least in terms of physical appearance. My initial response, that being a wide smile with both hands lifted in greeting, melted away like an ice-cube in the desert sun as the gangling monstrosities boogied clearly into view.

Point of order in case of '*Pretty Boy Floyd*': the former Arm ante suit/Rolex watch-wearing Slickster with the five-hundred dollar haircut and owner of a set of pearly white choppers that, when flashed within a bright aura at the correct angle, could equally mesmerize and/or blind, wobbled about like a drunken stumble- bum.

218

His normally oil-slick black hair stuck out in every possible direction like ink-stained rail spikes-both his lips had been eaten away, a tiny shred of the bottom one still clinging to his chin like a bloated slug. The only portion of his suit that hadn't been torn away was his right shirt sleeve and the left leg above the knee, while his white undershirt was soaked in a fiery kaleidoscope of dark red, bright yellow and puke green. As he lumbered closer, I noticed his left hand was void all fingers save the thumb, while his right eye socket had been hollowed out like a festive pumpkin.

The 'Profs' condition wasn't a hell of a lot better, though he had managed to retain the majority of his clothing. As for missing digits, et al, a sizeable portion of the man's nose had been gnawed away, as had the lobes of both ears. Worse yet, the center of his throat just above the Adam's Apple housed a golf- ball sized chasm that looked to have been punctured from the *inside*. Dancing forward in his stocking feet, Godale commenced to wail and groan through obviously damaged vocal cords, a greenish mist spewing from the wound like fizzy soda from the tab of a rigorously shaken tin-can.

I began to jog backward atop the slick pavement, though initially not fast enough to keep the grisly mob from gaining ground. Might sound callous since I never was quite sure of their intentions, but I wasn't about to saunter up and give either of 'em a hug. It wasn't until I noticed two of Honor-Guard's finest bringing up the rear minus miscellaneous limbs that the adrenals kicked in, thus increasing my pace substantially. As with

Gaven, Virgil, and the rest, all four possessed similarly bloated midsections, no doubt housing separate species of insect larvae; twin incubators that walked upright without the actual benefit of being alive in the logical sense.

Still unable to pry my eyes from the grisly phenomenon giving chase, I watched the four figures slow their pursuit as if giving up the chase. Pretty Boy Garrison bent over and balanced his hands atop his bare knees as if sucking some serious wind, while the Professor and the guard twins trudged along an additional two-dozen feet before joining suit. Taking their cue, I took the opportunity to catch my own breath as the distance between us grew to at least thirty or forty yards.

A few seconds later, while spitting free a thick wad of built-up phlegm to the shiny pavement, it became fairly obvious that fatigue had had little to do with my former employer's sudden halt. First off, Pretty Boy Garrison's throat blew up like a mutating toad frog, while the Prof reached up and clutched the sides of his skull as if suffering from the Mother of All migraines.

Secondly, the security twins began to shake and tremor as if standing on a squared section of active fault-line. Seriously, it was like watching a vaudeville act straight out of opening night in hell. Both of 'em were waggling about like partially dismembered G. I. Joe dolls, each minus an arm, while one was hopping about on a right leg missing the attached foot. It just seemed downright weird that both had managed to retain their helmets and heavily-tinted visors while sustaining so much other

220

bodily damage. Then again, after all I'd seen go down in that fiery pit and beyond, such visual lunacy was pretty much par course.

At almost precisely the moment that a gusher of mantis hatchlings erupted from Pretty Boy Garrison's outstretched jaws in a foamy torrent, Ron Godale's head and face exploded as if he'd previously swallowed a grenade minus the pin, coating his hands, arms and upper torso in a mushy combo of brain tissue, skull fragments, and bug puree. Both remained mostly upright, their hollowed husks falling to the pavement only after the mass evacuation of bugs that had been holding them up to begin with. I still couldn't quite grasp the species' 'eat and run' technique, but couldn't help but think of Beth suffering a similar fate and came damn near dry-heaving in the aftermath.

Fed up with the whole fucking freak show and long past the point of total exhaustion, I was about to pivot on a bare heel and shag ass in order to permanently place the Net-Scan Corporation and New Horizon's in my rear view mirror when I noticed the Honor-Guard twins had beat me to the punch. Both had turned tail and hauled off in the opposite direction, showing off surprising dexterity and speed despite their numerous mutilations. I noticed numerous hatchings left in their tracks, the glut of which fell from underneath their visors like finely chopped confetti.

Ridiculous as it sounds, I found myself downright offended by such behavior, and almost yelled out to them as if to confirm I'd been the source of their sudden exit.

Upon turning about as a loud scraping sound filled the dead air, the true origin of their fears scrambled forth directly into my path.

Though I'd misjudged her size a bit, no doubt due to the enormous birthing sac she'd been perched upon, the Queen was still one mammoth mama.

Crawling forth on multiple legs that hummed and sizzled like fired pistons, her dripping maw opened and closed continuously, while the twin pinchers snapped and cracked like small-arms fire. Obviously, I'd managed to touch a nerve with my douse and run exit from the pit, and she'd braved the surface solely in my honor.

Just for the record, one has never known the textbook definition of fear until they're being pursued by an eighteen-foot high Praying Mantis/Assassin Bug hybrid queen looking for some payback from the mortal man who'd wasted a few thousand of her precious offspring.

Then again, that armor-plated monstrosity born and bred from hell's deepest, darkest cavern was responsible for murdering the best friend I'd ever had, so vengeance was, at least in this case, definitely a two-way street. Sure she was pissed, but so was I, and for damn good reason. Problem was, and a monumental fucker it was, what exactly was I gonna do about it? I'd noticed a half-dozen or so 'pesticide-acid' burns on the underneath of her shell at the spot where the lower portion of the body segmented into the top. Sad to say, it didn't look as though the splashing of Demon-X had even penetrated beyond a few inches, and it wasn't as if I were piloting an M-1 tank loaded with nuke-laced missiles. On the contrary, I was a naked exterminator who'd been road hard and put away wet-clueless, weaponless, though not quite *gutless*, for whatever good that did me.

Once she got to within fifteen to twenty yards from where I stood frozen like a spooked Buck doused in floodlights, the Queen flung its beach-ball sized noggin airborne and released a sharp, piercing warrior's cry that snapped my daze and instantly reenergized the legs and feet. Talk about your instant motivation, I went from limping cripple to sprinting track star in a matter of blinks.

Exiting the paved roadway, I spotted a wide, metallic drainage pipe to my left, just past a series of skeletal condos consisting mostly of stone foundations that had yet to see further construction. Obviously newly placed, the gleaming pipe's top half had yet to be covered over, and trailed into a nearby hillside that I could only guess eventually led to a spillway of some type. All in all, just another case of 'not sure where I'd going, but I'm a headed that-a-way', an all-too-familiar scenario by that time.

The pipe was perhaps six and a half feet in height, just high enough so I wasn't forced to run scrunched over, and four or five feet wide. As had been the case since being so unceremoniously stripped of my New Horizon's 'Super-Exterminator' costume, I couldn't afford fretting as my bare feet splashed through the inch or so of fresh rainfall that had accumulated on the pipe's cool, slick surface. Damn thing could've been lined with upside down carpenter's tacks and I would've have known it 'til the bottom of my already bruised and bloodied dogs resembled pincushions. At least I wasn't running blind, as the tunnels uncovered ceiling was littered with enough nail and screw-holes to provide some indirect light. I could only guess I'd covered around a hundred yards, the last twenty or so on a slight upgrade, when the possibility of a collapsed lung forced a brief sabbatical. Never one for a regular exercise regimen, at least not since my high school days on the ol' round-ball team, it wasn't a stretch to claim I'd covered seven or eight miles worth of terrain since daybreak, the last two or three as a naked savage/throwback to the Neanderthal age. A true testament to man's power of endurance, fueled solely by an aversion to extinction. Run to live…live to run-flight over fight. Whatever preserved the precious hide, baby.

The drain grew dark just as I'd resumed the trek, a large shadow hovering overhead like an ominous storm-cloud, followed by a loud thumping directly overhead.

As the drain crumbled like a crushed tin-can less than a dozen feet ahead of me, I heard a familiar banshee-like cry. Not being able to fit into the drain, it seemed apparent that Big Mama had sniffed me out and essentially 'cut me off at the pass', so to speak. Give credit where credit is due, my man. Intelligent fucker, she was. Persistent as well-persistent…determined…one bad-ass skilled hunter-not to mention hell-bent on revenge. Backing from the abrupt dead-end, I barely flinched when the backside collapsed inward as well, this time within reaching distance of where I'd paused in mid-stride. Mama Big Claws cried out once again, this particular screech not as drawn out and a bit more subdued somehow...*smugly satisfied* might well fit the description best...as if her obligatory victory meal was merely moments away. Feeling a bit 'sardine-ish' to say the least, I backed up as far as the limited space would allow and hugged the wall between clinched shoulder blades while dropping to one knee.

"Hope ya choke on me, bitch!" I screamed once the slightly hooked tips of the Queen's pinchers pierced the ceiling less than two feet from the tip of my scalp. Not exactly original or clever-but then clever, ad-lib dialogue had always been Bethy's thing, not mine. As metal peeled away like so much soggy confetti, a few hundred of mama's recently hatched offspring toppled in all around me, scuttling around my ten by six prison suite like blind mice sniffing out a hunk of moldy cheese. As I busied myself swatting them off my feet, legs and arms, a coffin-sized chunk of the drain roof was stripped and tossed away. Rain-clouds had given way to blazing sunlight in the short time I'd played thief with the sacred ID of one Count of Monte Cristo.

Temporarily blinded by the abrupt intrusion, I had just whacked one of the little bastards from the head of my severely shriveled manhood when a brief, shrill hum filled the space, followed by what sounded like a deep, pain-fueled sigh. Within seconds, the entirely of Big Mama Claws' child army had backed from me like finicky felines from a bowl of soured milk. A few ticks more, and they'd all crawled topside amid a short, terrifying stretch of deafening silence.

The message was resoundingly clear: when it comes to mealtime, Hive Queens *do not* partake in sloppy seconds.

I stood cautiously, blocking the basking sunlight with a raised forearm as a cool breeze streaked through the drain's ravaged roof. Following an additional thirty to forty-five ticks without further movement or sound, I had begun to cultivate false hope that perhaps Big Bag Mama had flown the coup and taken the kiddies with her. Sad to confess, but even the most ridiculous of pipe dreams can seem logical in the light of complete exhaustion. I'd taken several half-steps forward, until just a fraction of my head and torso felt sudden warmth from direct sun contact when the queen's beach-ball sized head filled the space like a full eclipse.

Falling back, I fell into the crumpled metal, scraping the back of my skull and upper back on bent, jagged steel. Fade to black amidst the revolting sound of the Queen shoving her bulk into the drain.

Awakened, my eyes flittered and remained an unfocused blur, that is until I'm able to identify the gain pincher posed less than six inches from my face-a pincher the size of a crane hook that flexed and un-flexed as if warming up for an impending workout. Involuntarily tilting my head 'til it leaned hard left, I caught a glimpse of the Hive Queen's inquisitive mug, its roving right eye taking in the

226

whole of me as if I were a prize catch indeed. Unlike before, I couldn't even muster the motivation nor energy for a clever exiting speech. I heard a hissing, guttural growl and the pincher unflexed, pulling its twin hooks wide in a pre-strike stretch.

Thank merciful God, my vision faded just as the razor-edged appendage shot forward.

BUG OUT, PART FOURTEEN

Shock Therapy

Come to with a startled jolt. My teeth gnash with such force that my tongue detects the metallic taste of chewed filling fragments. The space is well lit from a line of fluorescent bulbs hanging from each corner of the tiny, squared room. Blinking rapidly as to eliminate the sporadic blurriness handicapping my vision, I detect the faint scent of disinfectant. Spitting out three small chunks of silver filling onto the white sheet covering my lower extremities, only then do I notice the IV line taped to the inside elbow of my left arm. I lift the sheet and sneak a quick peak. Though not quite nude, I am donned in only a pair of maroon boxer shorts and V-necked cotton tee, the latter of which is soaked in fresh sweat. In peering down at my right forearm, something catches my tearing eye and I find myself executing a double-take at an altogether unfamiliar tattoo located there-a faded nautical anchor with the words 'U. S. S Wyoming' stenciled in below it. Still dazed as hell, there is a sense of bewilderment that is overwhelming. At first sight, everything appears weirdly alien, not the least of which are my very own appendages. My forearms seem too thin…painfully gaunt, while each hand looks obscenely large, the digits almost spidery in appearance. I start to raise the sheet in order to check my feet when a door opens and almost instantly suctions itself closed, followed by a flurry of footsteps echoing off hard, tiled flooring.

Footsteps that grow ever closer, accompanied by whispering voices whose dialogue soon graduate from inaudible gibberish to at least partially comprehensible.

"Oh, you're awake. Very good," the first says cheerily with a stout cockney accent, its originator a medium-sized male wearing an ankle-length lab coat. Damn if the man, middle-aged and with the accompanying spread near his mid-section, isn't vaguely familiar, though for the life of me I can't yet drudge up a name to go with the partially blurred face. Perhaps once my vision is completely cleared, a tried and true cord will be struck.

"We figured your afternoon nap to be a good half-hour from completion," the second, a thick-bodied African-American man, adds in a deep baritone voice that is, once again, oddly familiar.

"How are we feeling this afternoon?"

The first man steps closer, a lengthy clipboard clasped to his chest by folded arms, and spots the discarded filler fragments.

"Uh-oh. Looks as though we've experienced yet another rim-sleep incident, doctor."

The second joins him, and both stand less than two feet from the left side of the bed frame.

"Ah, I see. Well, the side-effects of the…multiple treatments we've administered can be quite extreme upon re-entering the sometimes harsh realm of reality."

Several dozen more blinks and I'm finally able to focus on the two faces peering downward at me like some recently altered lab specimen.

"Despite such episodes, I'd still maintain that you're right on schedule for early release," the first blurts excitedly while freeing the clipboard from indenture as to flip through its tightly clamped pages.

The second man chimes in just as I'm able to clearly ID the first, my lips parting to scream out but finding little in the way of lung power to complete the act.

"Oh, no doubt about that…next Thursday, isn't it? Why, I see no reason why a clean bill of health isn't in order her-…."

I cut him off, this second recognizable figure, with a frantic wave of my left arm as the IV line pops free and winds around its metal-pole host like a constricting reptile.

"J-Jesus…Jesus Lord…h-how? How can y-you…you two…what is…d- don't I know y-you…what is…is this? Where am…am…

WHAT THE HELL IS GOING ON?"
Strange…my very own voice rings untrue, unrecognizable in both tone and accent.

Neither man steps back an iota, or even cringes slightly for that matter, as if such a frantic reaction was expected. They do share a meaningful glance…meaningful that is, for all within the tiny space save yours truly. The stoutly built black man, he of the barrel-shaped chest, tree-trunk thick biceps and no-neck appearance, winks playfully and begins to speak in a low, condescending tone that makes me want to reach up and tear out his fucking eyes.

"Now, now…just take a deep breath and calm down. Everything is as it should be, though I

230

understand the complexities to the unclear mind. Give it a few minutes and it'll come to you…I promise."

"Come…come to me?" I rant, feeling the pulse at my neck and temples throb like trip-hammers.

"Suppose I'm not too quick on the uptake and one of you 'in-the-know' assholes kindly explains it to me?"

Again, the two exchange a knowing glance as my jaw muscles commence to re-tighten, threatening whatever dental work that still remains.

"What? Didn't I say *pretty-please*? Spill, Goddammit!"

The pot-bellied Brit responds first, his pity-filled expression pissing me off ever farther.

"Before we…delve into today's initial question and answer segment, do me a favor, will you? Just think…concentrate…see if you can tell us why *you* think you're here?"

Figuring that humoring these pompous ass-wipes was the only way I was ever going to get a straight answer, I manage to defuse my volcanic temper via a few deep breaths.

"Truthfully, gents, I have no idea how I got wherever 'here' is. My memories are a bit…fragmented at the moment." No-neck speaks up next, his nostrils flaring as if he'd just picked up a stout scent. Damn, but he looks *so* familiar. Both do, in fact, and more so with each passing tick of the clock-my personal head-shrink *tag-team*, perhaps?

"What say I provide a refresher then…see if it…rings any bells, so to speak?"

231

"By all means," I shrug, eyeing a thick, clear liquid leak ever-so-gradually from where the IV line left a tiny hole at my elbow,"refresh away, doc."

As the pot-bellied Brit stands stoically by the bedside, his expression as bland as the puke-green paint adorning the four walls, no-neck begins to pace the limited space with the tip of his chin rested atop a curled fist.

"Very well then, we'll play it by word association. I'll give you the clue...you attempt to...fill in the blank."

I nod without speaking, a deep-seeded itch building steam near the elbow wound and also, inexplicably, at my ankles and feet. Must be whatever drug they have me hopped up on wearing down 'til the next treatment.

"Alright then...let's start with...*New Horizons*." New...Horizons? A bell does sound, though pitifully faint at best.

"New...um...a corporation of some sort, I take it. Computers maybe?

Software? One of those chip factories in Southern Calif-..." Pot-Belly politely waves me off and No-Neck resumes."How about...*Honor Guard*?"

Again, only a slight buzzing at best-much like the two bozos performing the bedside interrogation, something lies just below the surface I can't quite grasp.

"Uh...some sort of...soldiering outfit, like Rangers or Paratroopers...though mercenary in nature."

232

"Not...quite there, but on the right track," No-Neck replies with a condescending smirk. Where ever I do know this clown from, I get the feeling I never liked 'im.

"Alright then, allow me to break out the heavy artillery. Does the term... 'Hive Queen' mean anything to you?" Jesus, like a dark blue, streaking bolt of lighting penetrating soft brain tissue-'*Hive Queen*'...images scream into my mind at warp speed-'*Hive Queen*'...images both pleasant and grim-graven and horrific-'*Hive* Fucking *Queen*'- suddenly I see it all in High Definition quality-hear it all in ear-piercing Dolby. '*Hive Queen*'...I witness...no, make that *relive*...so much misery...so much death...including...including what appears to be...my very own.

"Ah-ha..." blurts Pot-Belly while slowly flipping through pages on his clipboard,"seems we've struck a nerve, doctor."

No-Neck confirms with a playful wink as the itching sensation grows stronger at my calves and ankles.

"Yes, indeed, rather like the tip of an ice-pick into an open wound, I'd say."

"Hi-hive Queen...so...so you know? B-both of y-you...know..."

No more anger...the building rage had vanished as the body and mind began a gradual meltdown. It's a damn wonder I can speak at all. They knew my story...somehow they knew. But then, how did I escape that drain intact...and...get here...with them?

"Yes, we know the story, good sir," Pot-Belly mocks, his broad grin revealing short, stubby teeth stained a shade dark possibly from decades of both heavy smoking and black coffee consumption.

"Lord knows we've been exposed to it's rather…lurid details on countless occasions."

No-Neck practically guffaws, tossing his melon-shaped head back like a baying wolf.

"Damned right we have, doctor. By now I can practically recite it…backwards and forwards…verbatim…in my sleep. Hell, practically in *your* sleep."

He turns his attention back to me, his maniacal grin having instantly faded into oblivion and replaced by an angry sneer. I swear I see a line of frothy spittle fly from his lips as he resumes.

"Truth is…and be advised that I'm well aware of the healing oath I've taken as a physician…if I hear one more tall tale concerning mutated bugs from Earth's core prepping to consume the planet like a great big Caesar salad…. (he pauses to wring his hands)… I'll be damned tempted to strangle somebody with their IV line, how about you, Doctor?"

"Agreed in principal, doctor. Time for a bit of…tough love, I believe, specifically for those hiding behind a facade of fictional fear to snap to and join the rest of functional society."

Pot-Belly leans over and glares at me through tightly-squinted eyes, the clipboard again jammed to his chest like a bulletproof vest.

234

"The jig is most certainly up, Mister Jenkins, or are we safely cloaked in an alternate personality today?"

"Mister Jen-. ." I mutter, and spot the black-stenciled words spelled out on the back of the clipboard for the first time. I read them several times, probably aloud, though I cannot be certain. It reads:

Virgil Hobbs Psychiatric Center, Waco, Texas

"Talk to me, good sir. Am I speaking to Wilt Jenkins or someone else? Please identify yourself."

The two men continue to exchange dialogue, some directed towards me and the rest towards each other, only a fraction of which I actually comprehend.

Virgil Hobbs Center? What does it mean? Hobbs had a loony ward named after him, for Christ's sake? When did this happen? I've heard of some wacky memorials in my time, but why would a mental institution be named after a dead exterminator?

"Come now, Wilt," No-Neck brays, waving his arms about like a carnival barker from centuries past. I begin to think there are secret cameras hidden about the room, placed solely to record the individual performances, ala 'reality TV'.

"Dare I have to cover the entire checklist?" Despite strident efforts to keep it at bay, the anger arises anew, fueled mostly by the 'doctors' arrogant attitudes and casual indifference to my plight.

"Checklist? What the hell are you talking about? Who's this…*Wilt* you keep mentioning, and what do you mean, identify yourself? Don't either of you…professional *jackasses* know who I am?"

"Depends on the day, Wilt," Pot-Belly responds, joining his muscle-bound cohort at the head of the bed. The *Mockery Brothers*, front and center-if I had the strength I'd take 'em both on, present injuries be damned.

"Sometimes even on the time of day."

I shrug impatiently as if to indicate for the idiot to further elaborate, all the while scratching around the IV wound like a flea-infested mutt.

Yet another smarmy glance ensues between the two before No-Neck officially gets the nod as Pot-Belly fades to the background.

"In a nutshell, Wilt, our…team has endured your fantastic story concerning mutated assassin bugs and the impending Armageddon for going on seven months now. Action-packed, horror-filled blockbuster that it is, I'm afraid the plain, unvarnished truth behind your stay here at the institute is minus the majority of the Sci-Fi trappings, though equally terrifying in many aspects."

Seven…*months*? As in two-hundred blessed days, give or take? Is this moron serious?

"So…I've been in a coma, is that what you're saying?"

"Not in the least," Pot-Belly exclaims before handing the reigns back over to No-Neck with an amiable nod.

"Continuous treatment, Mister Jenkins, to include extensive, daily therapy sessions, the majority of which we two (he turns to Pot-Belly, who actually bows, for cripes sake…grins like the village idiot and *bows*) personally spearheaded."

With a splitting headache now accenting the infernal full-body itching, my patience meter officially peters out.

"Y'know, it's great you assholes are having such a knee-slapping good time at my expense…now how about cutting to the fucking chase before we all just dust away?"

"I see we've now entered the 'denial *slash* rage' phase," No-Neck replies sternly, aggressively crossing those Anaconda-sized arms across one another.

"Fine then, Wilt, the condensed version, though it'll be us 'assholes' who'll be forced to deal with the cataclysmic aftermath in terms of the meltdown sure to follow."

I stare muscles down and refuse to blink, though my hands and upper body shake uncontrollably.

"I can take it, Ace. Talk to me…"

"You suffer from several post-traumatic disorders, Mister Jenkins, from which there appears to be no permanent cure. These disorders originated and gestate within your subconscious mind due to the tragic events of seven months past, wherein you bore witness to the brutal murders of several co-workers."

"Can't argue with ya there, Chief," I reply with a mock salute, "so far…so good."

237

Ignoring my less-than-flattering gesture, No-Neck trudges on unabated."Victims are listed as Gaven Alan McCloud, Delbert Carl Prescott, Gilbert Milton Braggs, James Jay Bohannon and...last but certainly not least...one Jack Ray Barton." The air catches in my lungs like liquid fire...the burning tingling at my scalp a worthy counterpart in misery to the incessant itching already in progress.

"Jack...Jack Barton you say? I...um...I'm afraid...t-the comprehension train just derailed...b-big time...."

Pieces of a maddening puzzle, though still randomly scattered, begin to fall methodically into place. Even as my wondering, spastic gaze switches back and forth between each man, an overwhelming sense of Déjà vu threatens to render me unconscious-Déjà vu possibly in cahoots with a mind-state far more sinister. I *know* these two pricks, damn it, so why in God's name can't I place them?

"Yes, Wilt...Jack Barton. The same Jack Barton you often claim to *be* during...an episode such as this. The same Jack Barton that you otherwise claim to have been your co-worker and business partner for the past seven years, that is, until the incident that took his life and the others. Jack Barton, also known as your best friend-a friend who once served as best man at your wedding."

Wedding? Begs the question-who exactly did I marry?

"Afraid you…you're striking out on all counts, Ace. This here boy's… (pause to catch a much-needed breath) a life-long bachelor…confirmed."

"We have a copy of the marriage certificate in your file, Wilt," Pot-Belly exclaims blandly. Man loves positively bored. Meanwhile, my lower abdomen flutters and I feel the initial symptoms of an impending cramp.

"Her name, Ace…clue me in."

No-Neck interludes once again, although mercifully his gestures are no longer animated in the least.

"Beth. Beth Cambridge Jenkins. You were married almost eight years ago at a small church in your hometown of Abilene."

Aw, that seriously fucking hurts. Ice-pick to the testicles type pain. Excruciating in the extreme. Sticking a live electrical wire to moistened lips would positively tickle by comparison. My stomach rolls…my entire fucking body is now a ripe boil awaiting a razor-edged blade to spill its pus-filled contents.

"Correction, doctors. Beth is…. was my spraying partner. We never…that is, we were close but never, ever got within close proximity to a church alter. The…(pause yet again for a fresh lungful)…you guys really need to think of replacing that crack research staff. . ."

"Mister Jenkins, Beth…your wife signed the papers to have you…committed. She… had you placed with us, understand?"

"Committed for what? For trying to warn the free world of the apocalypse to come? I know what

239

I saw down there…and in the very streets of New Horizons…I felt the pain…smelled the blood…the shredded viscera. I. . . wa-…(catch my breath, which hitches after every fourth or fifth word)…I was…I had to warn 'em…warn somebody…"

"Wilt, listen to me carefully now, and try to concentrate your thoughts on what I'm about to say. Picture it in your mind-allow the thought process to flow naturally. Try to recall," Pot-Belly whispers, handing the clipboard to No-Neck, who fades into the background with his head turned away and nodding solemnly.

"Recall a late afternoon excursion to a closed-down sports complex. An excursion dictated by workload. Your team enters and accidentally steps directly in the line of fire as a gang-related killing is taking place. All die save one, a former marine nicknamed 'Kong' for his oversized hands and naturally clumsy nature. You see, the man named 'Kong' had possessed an inner rage long-since dormant since his combat days with the core. That night, the rage is awakened, and the man named Kong begins to recall the killing skills he'd long since abandoned as a mild-mannered exterminator. Kong kills all four of the protagonists with sadistic glee, yet is immediately tortured by the guilt that his brutal acts of retribution might not have been necessary if only he'd showed similar courage earlier in the night."

The Pot-Bellied Brit places a clammy hand atop my bare shoulder and squeezes ever-so-slightly. It's a comforting feeling, if for no other reason than to soothe the itch there. As for the speech, it's nothing more than a severely condensed version of one I'd heard recently from the mouth of Gaven McCloud…the campfire ghost tale to end all bug-stomper tales. That is…until now.

"There are no mutated bugs from earth's core, Wilt. There *never* was. There was no fiery pit buried beneath the fictional New Horizons sub-division, since there is no such company to speak of, nor a sub-division. There was no Hive Queen, as there is no such hive. You're here, Wilt, with us. You're here…to heal, so that you may resume a normal existence. It's what your wife…what Beth wants. It's what she prays for. We're here to help you…and your wife…see that prayer answered."

"Beth…put me here? That's…bull-…(I'm forced to pause from the effects of a severe stomach cramp)…bullshit (it eases off as I break into a cold, sticky sweat)…as for your so-called reason, G-Gaven McCloud told me that same story at the New Horizon's in-brief. What the hell's going on here, anway? Who's behind this…this…colossal skull-fuck?"

"Correction, Wilt," No-Neck concludes in a solemn tone, having taken up position on the other side of the bed, opposite Pot-Belly,"Gaven McCloud was murdered within that same story…a story that falls, unfortunately, under the heading of non-fiction."

Pot-Belly speaks, and I twist around to face him.

"It really happened, Mister Jenkins. Our mission is to get you to face that sad, horrible truth,

241

and learn to deal with it so you may get on with the rest of your life."

No-Neck takes another turn-my head spins his way.

"The institute director, Doctor Hobbs, has instructed us to increase therapy time while decreasing your medication. Episodes such as this, I'm afraid, are the consequence."

As a fresh coating of sour-smelling sweat coats my face, neck and arms, I feel my scalp ignite as if soaked in kerosene and lit ablaze with a flame-thrower. As I speak, my throat burns with equal fervor. As for the maddening itch, it dominates my lower half like a flesh-eating bacteria with an insatiable appetite.

"Crock of horse-shit. I *know* who…who I am…who I've…been. I know what I saw, and what I…what I lived through. You two can…take your half- baked…diagnosis…dia-…diagnosis and s-shove it where your anal ther- thermometer outta be…I…. goddammit! You claim to be…m-men of medicine, correct? Well th-then, can you *please* do something…anything to relive…relieve this infernal itching?"

Hugging myself, I use the overgrown fingernails of both hands to dig fresh trenches into my sides, upper shoulders and forearms before delving into the lower regions to my groin and inner thighs. Temporarily distracted by the inane misery of it all, I consciously neglect the doctor's Grimm as they trade opinions and/or suggestions on how to ease my wretched plight. Their movements are fuzzy blurs; their words meaningless drivel.

Having effectively shredded several layers of flesh from both forearms, I glance up and over at Pot-Belly, who continues to chat casually even as infant Assassin Bugs fly off his tongue, erupt from both nostrils and violently spurt from each eye like pus-sacs from a mashed zit. In-turn, No-Neck reacts and replies accordingly, seemingly paying no mind to the divisions of hard-shelled insects scuttling from his every orifice like lava from an active volcano.

"But...weeeeee can't increeeassse the m-m-meds...Hobb's diiiiii-rect orrrrd-deerrrrr, rememmm-memburrrrrrrr?" Pot-Belly garbles between crunching chews, bug guts coating his chin in a yellowish hue. His neck bulges and recedes with clockwork efficiency as a new horde rise for impending extraction.

"I'mmmm...at a...lossssssss heeeerrrrreeeee...thiisssss man issssssss hope-lesssssss-ly crackkkkkkkkkked," No-Neck argues as countless masses spew from each ear and several dozen others find liberation via a dime-sized hole dug into his bald dome.

As both men are unceremoniously charted away to be dined upon by the very armies they themselves birthed, their ceaseless banter never wavers. As I sat squirming and wriggling like an earthworm on a fisherman's hook, I see Pot-Belly's eyeballs pop free and roll across the shiny linoleum floor like discarded marbles. Subsequently, No-Neck has left both an arm (the right) and foot (the left) behind, the formers attached hand still gripping a finely chewed number two pencil.

My legs tremble and shake like a heroin addict in detox, and I peer down to see a wide, dark stain spreading below each knee. The doctors' nonsensical, unintelligible babbling ends as their transformation from human being to human compost heap nears a final, fatal turn. From my perspective, they resemble statues carved from black marble; only this particular cut of marble pulsates with life not simply from two heartbeats, but untold thousands.

I grip the sheet near my thighs with shaking hands; hands suddenly swarming with clear, pimple-like blisters.

A swift, forceful jerk and the sheet sails away like a hovering apparition.

I soak in two distinct scenes before the lights begin to dim. Two scenes I pray to god will not follow me to the afterlife like some cursed rerun to be relived for all eternity. The first, and arguably least of the two horrors due only to the fact it is the first to be revealed:

The surrealistic picture of what had been my lower legs, ankles and feet, having metamorphosed into the prickly, armored plated appendages of the dreaded Assassin Bug, complete with a trio of clawed toes per foot. If nothing else, this certainly explains the maddening itch.

The second, and if possible, infinitely more shocking: Peeking to my right with eyes a-boggle and mouth agape, I catch a glimpse of my own terror-struck reflection in a nearby mirror. Ah-hah! Bells of familiarity ring loud and true! I recognize that face, damn it! Ah yes, I know it well! A familiar face, just as I'd suspected…and most certainly not the butt-ugly mug of this Wilt Jenkins character! Julie Barton's little boy, that's who I be, like there was ever any doubt.

Alas, such celebrations can be damned foolhardy, however, not to mention woefully premature. As it is, my warped grin fades to a slack-jawed grimace…

…. as a battalion of ravenous offspring spew from each nostril and leap from my exposed tongue like paratroopers from a plane's open hatch.

The room fades to a dim grayish fog…I feel the sticky warmth trail down my cheeks and an uncomfortable pressure at my sinus cavities…

All goes abruptly dark as the ravenous little bastards push their way out into the open air via the last pair of virgin orifices available…I hear two distinct plopping sounds, followed by what can only be described as marbles being rolled across a hardwood floor. Trembling fingers search in the gloom and bury themselves knuckle-deep into the hollowed sockets which remain.

I think I scream…or at least mimic the act…however pathetic…however futile… before…before…the inevitable…. the end…of it…all…

EPILOGUE

Meet the New Boss...

I wake in a shaken, groggy stupor, having reached up with unsteady hands to ensure my eyes are still indeed intact. Mercifully, they are, though it's hardly a given that's a good thing at this particular juncture. Rubbing them vigorously with slime-coated fingers, I begin a series of hard rolls from side to side and rapid blinking in hopes of reigniting the inner pilot light, so to speak. A familiar reeking is present, like raw, shredded entrails. I can only pray the stench originates from some nearby source and not from...well, you know.

More than anything else related to this Kafkaesque nightmare-more than grisly imagery of hollowed-out corpses and the stench of rotted flesh-more than the discovery that I alone carry the burden of survival within what had been an elite gathering of exterminators--even more than playing hapless prey to a seemingly unstoppable predator-more than the wretched dreams that drain away what little sanity remains-I grow so...very...goddamned tired of the darkness.

It's only when the pod-sac collapses and I fall through the tear, landing atop cold, jagged rock with a teeth-jarring thud that I realize my eye-sight hadn't been the problem after all. Takes a few ticks, but the old orbs come to life in high def glory.

Oh...shit. . . then again, there are times when total blindness would be the preferred choice.

As bad as that loony-bin ward dream had been, complete with Doctors Prescott and Bohannon in residency and the multiple ID switches, it doesn't hold a fucking candle to cold, hard reality. In truth, I'd give my left nut to be gallivanting around some alternate universe as Wilt 'Kong' Jenkins right about now, although if truth be told the monetary worth of the ol' family jewels can't amount to much about how.

From the hideously bloated belly and equally repulsive shrunken lower torso, I can only guess the gestation cycle calls for feeding on the most muscular appendages for protein before nesting in the upper to await an official birthing sequence. My thighs and calves look to have been sucked dry from the inside...no doubt a pretty accurate description that-flesh, bone and little else.

Arms aren't exactly in buffed mode either, both resembling horribly emaciated, vein-encased vines-the attached hands skeletal with gnarled, purple-shaded fingers. Rolling over onto my left side with Herculean effort, no thanks to the rubber limb brigade, I noticed a few toes missing from each foot. Guess you'd call that 'tissue-rot'. Explains all the involuntary amputees I've seen wondering about. It's a medical fact, I'd presume; digits have a tendency to fall away if not provided adequate nourishment and/or the required circulation.

The bastards circle me like coyotes to fresh road-kill, though none actually make contact. Guess it's one of Big Mama's unwritten rules none of the younger set dare to challenge-don't fuck with the miracle of birth.

Honestly, though I can't drudge up much to be thankful for, at least I don't have to feel the effects of my body unhinging like a doll with loose screws. It seems somewhere between the drain capture and subsequent relocation back to the Queen's pit, I've gone completely numb, much like one's jaw after a particularly messy visit to the dentist's chair. Must be part of their gestation checklist, to ensure the host is sufficiently doped up as to produce a healthy litter.

I hear Big Mama roar out in three to five second intervals and manage to roll back over to face the music, so to speak. She brought me here for a reason, and not just to see her latest batch burst free. She brought me here to see…something else. Don't ask me how…I just know this to be fact. Perhaps I'm labeled special since I avoided the abominable process longer than the others. Perhaps it's due to the fact that my impromptu cleansing with the flusher unit wasted so many of her young and she has a point to make in the aftermath. Whatever…I see what she wants me to see-it isn't as if the meaning behind it is so deeply profound. Jack Barton ain't no brain-surgeon, but even mutilated, crippled and impregnated with mutant Assassin Bug offspring, he isn't King Dumb-Shit either. Like the old saying goes, it doesn't take a load of bricks to fall on this boy's noggin to get the point across. Beth might've argued that point.

Sweet, stubborn Bethy-as before, my thoughts travel a winding road towards sickly sentimentality. Can't help it…ours was the closest relationship I'd ever known. Perhaps a reunion is impending-a reunion, lord forgive the cliché, held in a much better place.

A massive gathering of what appears to be a mixed bag of cockroach species, everything from German to American to the reclusive Brown-Banded type, are herded into a tight circle not three feet from where I lay. They topple and trample one another, but are prevented from fleeing a set perimeter by a grouping of the larger Assassins.

The Queen and I lock gazes, her atop her mountainous sac and I the latest fatality in her quest for surface domination. With a single wave of her gigantic right pincher and an accompanying growl, the roach-herding sentinels fall upon the retreating mass like vultures on a blood-soaked carcass.

The carnage is over in less than a minute, I'd surmise, though an accurate count is far beyond me. I find both space and time matter very damn little in this new, alternate universe.

The Queen roars her approval and the feeding predators scuttle away, leaving behind scant roach remains save several shell fragments and the occasional severed leg or shattered antennae. I see her rise from her anointed throne and lumber my way at precisely the moment my midsection begins a session of intense cramping, forcing me to flip onto my back in pure, immeasurable agony-just when I thought I was beyond such physical anguish.

She leans over me, balanced on a sextuplet of heavily armored stilt-legs, this Queen of all she surveys, and points a hooked pincher at the very spot where the roach sacrifice was made.

The grin that follows speaks volumes in any language, be it man or insect in origin. Ah yes, Big Mama…message delivered loud and clear…still another age- old theory of man, the soon-to-be former dominant species of planet earth, bites the big one…

…as it now seems damned obvious roaches WILL NOT be Earth's lone survivor after all…

…Yep, there's a new bug Sheriff in town…and he's setting up shop for the duration…

As my chest implodes and my bloated throat pulsate and throb with new life of the six-legged variety, a wide shadow hovers overhead…the Queen balances the jagged, cloven claw above my head-waiting for the final few stragglers to exit the V-shaped chasm at my breastbone before dropping the hammer.

Thank god the quality of mercy is not limited solely to mankind… A final thought, or perhaps 'wish' is more appropriate:

Wherever afterlife for which I'm fated, I can only hope that it's naturally… pest-free…

THE END